THE WITCH
OF
BASTANÈS

DAN SCANNELL

Black Rose Writing | Texas

ISBN: 978-1-68433-986-0
PUBLISHED BY BLACK ROSE WRITING
www.blackrosewriting.com

Printed in the United States of America
Suggested Retail Price (SRP) $19.95

The Witch of Bastanès is printed in Garamond

*As a planet-friendly publisher, Black Rose Writing does its best to eliminate unnecessary waste to reduce paper usage and energy costs, while never compromising the reading experience. As a result, the final word count vs. page count may not meet common expectations.

I wish to express my thanks to Dr. Susan Fay, Professor Emeritus at Marymount University, for her encouragement and guidance. I extend a heartfelt thanks to Jefferson, my editor, to my wife, Laura and to my daughters, Susan and Sarah, for their faith, their patience and their hard work.

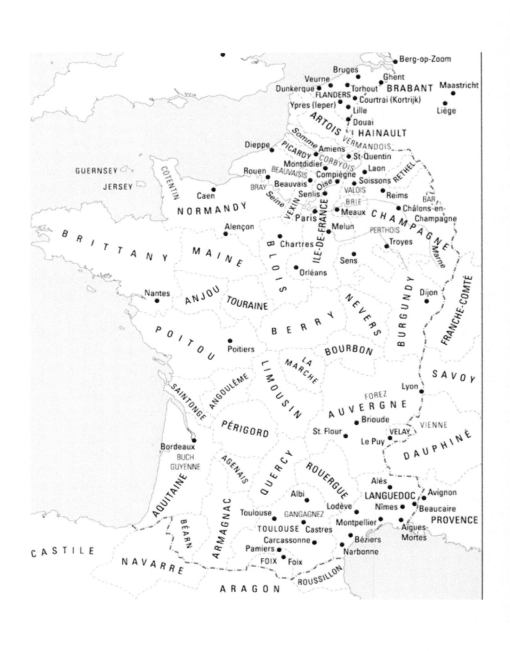

THE WITCH
OF
BASTANÈS

PROLOGUE

To the reader,

Every village in rural France has its colorful collection of folklore, passed down from the mists of the past. My grandmother came from a little collection of thatched-roofed houses, called Bastanès, in the French Pyrenees Mountains, not far from present day Pau. Here, they tell a tale of courage and love, no doubt partly fanciful and partly true, about a woman named Teresa and the man of some historical significance, with whom she shared a forbidden love. While visiting there, I was treated to a present-day version of the story.

When I returned to Paris, I spent the next three years searching for clues, amid the scant documents left from the turbulence of the thirteenth century, in an effort to piece together the facts behind this elaborately embroidered legend.

There were many gaps in the fragmentary historical record, which I was forced to fill with my own supposition and, at times fertile imagination. Permit me to share, with you, what I have concluded.

Limoux, (Southern France), July 7, 1220

My Dearest Teresa,

I am scribbling this to you, my little one, because your father and I shall not live to see the dawn. We will not be there to see you married or to know your children. We will never hold them or kiss them or share with them all we have seen and experienced. It pains me to think of you, a mere child of ten, alone in the world, fighting only to survive. How I wish that your father and I might still be at your side to guide and protect you from the wickedness of this world.

You see, the tales we told you about your grandpa and about why we had to leave the land and home we loved were not the whole truth. You are so young that we thought we could shelter you from the horrors people commit against one another when fear and hatred grip their hearts. We didn't tell you the whole truth, but now you must know, to keep yourself safe from the calamities that have befallen your family.

Flee. Flee before it is too late! War has filled men's eyes with blood, their hearts with fear and loathing. They seek me out because I am a Jewess, even though I love the Lord better than those who slaughter, in His name, anyone they perceive as different from themselves. They seek the Cathar heretics, but they will kill anyone, in the fever of holy war. I begged your father not to go to them, to plead on my behalf. They will only add him to the rolls of the dead; then they will seek me out. You must not be here, when they arrive, and I cannot go with you. Anyone with me is in danger. You must go, and you must go alone, as far as the narrow mountain passes will lead you.

I shall not apologize for loving your father, despite the gulf between our faiths. We loved your grandfather, as if he were father to us both. The wisdom that your father and I shared, at Papa's feet, would fill many libraries in earlier times. Those were the days when God was truly smiling upon all of us.

You should have been there, my love, when Toledo was a city of learning and splendor, filled with beautiful libraries, palaces, mosques, churches, and synagogues! Scholars from all around the world: Muslims, Christians, and our own rabbis, gathered together under Archbishop Raymond to translate the lost works of Aristotle, Ibn Rushd and others from Arabic, Hebrew and Greek into Latin, so that learned men of the West could read them. Your grandfather was, perhaps, the most distinguished of those rabbis. He taught me so many things and so many languages, that I could read all the books of philosophy, theology, astronomy, mathematics and especially medicine, herbal medicine, practiced by the ancient Greeks and handed down for centuries.

Your father was one of the young Christian scholars who chose to study under Papa. Fernando was tall and handsome, but, above all, he had an overwhelming hunger and love of learning. He would sit at Papa's feet for hour after hour, he a mathematician and Papa a numerologist, and discuss the patterns of numerical sequences and their implications. Fernando read Hebrew as well as Papa read Greek, so they joined like two spices in a soup, both different, both enriching each other.

The problem, of course, was me. I too possessed a passion for learning and had read widely on the subject. Papa encouraged me to participate in the discissions, and I did. Over time, I came to grips, not only with a difficult subject, but with my growing love for Fernando. When he confessed to me that he felt the same way about me, we plucked up the courage to ask Papa if we could be married.

Papa was reluctant, not because he did not love Fernando like a son. He respected the faith and traditions of our community, and he knew, with an awful certainty, what would happen to the Jews of Toledo, if our two communities came into conflict over this decision.

Finally, Papa relented, on condition that I would be permitted to keep my faith. Papa assured us that he was on friendly terms with several clerical scholars at the cathedral. He would arrange for a secret marriage, in the cathedral vestibule, after hours. Fernando and I would have to be discrete about living together as man and wife, so as not to draw undo attention to the situation.

Everything went according to plan, for the first three months. We moved about as if we were walking on eggshells. No one seemed to be the wiser, and we thought we had gotten away with it. That was when the world began to crumble beneath our feet.

I was only beginning to show, but the priest, who married us, was troubled in conscience and told his confessor. The confessor divulged what he had heard to the archbishop. Although our priest friend thought he had spoken *in the strictest confidence, the archbishop immediately consulted with the chief rabbi of the city. By vespers, that evening, all Toledo was buzzing with the news.*

The chief rabbi counselled patience from his community, and the archbishop called upon his flock to exercise calm. Nevertheless, a mob of mostly youthful hotheads from the Christian quarter, seeing a pretext for some mischief, made for the Jewish quarter, with torches and pitchforks in hand.

They smashed into homes and places of business, looting anything they could carry and burning the rest. They torched synagogues and shredded scrolls of the sacred Torah. Their unchecked rampage threatened to burn the Jewish quarter to cinders.

Papa, Fernando and I stuffed as much as we could into an old, wooden trunk and rushed out back to load it onto the aching haunches of Papa's old donkey. I could see, in his eyes, that the beast knew very well what all this meant: travel, long travel over mountainous roads, with little or no food or drink for many miles. The donkey looked around. Was this one of the rabbi's jaunts in search of some academic colleague or another? As we pulled the fastening ropes tighter, the smell of fear he detected from our overheated bodies told him that it was something different.

At the last minute, I rushed into the house and seized one of Fernando's collection of books. I refused to leave everything of value behind. I clutched it to my breast and expanding stomach. There was still room for me and the book on the donkey's back, and, after Fernando helped me to my place, we lurched out into the night.

We traveled over mountain passes for days and days, stopping occasionally only for food and rest. We ate hastily and departed before too many people had a chance to ask us any questions. Our tiny caravan passed endless fields of sheep and grass, with the occasional abandoned barn or farmhouse where we could stay for the night. It was at such a farmhouse that Papa, unable to mask the agony of hopelessness and regret that I could see in his face, succumbed to his weariness, and died.

Fernando and I only stayed long enough to give our patriarch a proper burial. We continued our journey until we detected a subtle change in the local dialect being trumpeted in the marketplaces. We noted, too, that the peaks of the mountains were behind, and not in front of us. Then, and only then, did we think of settling down and trying to achieve some semblance of a normal family life.

Huddled away, in a haphazard collection of sheep farms, my time arrived, and I gave birth to you, our very own brown eyed, dark haired little girl. Fernando and I remembered the promise we had given to the priest at our wedding. We took you to the village church, had you baptized and gave you the name Teresa.

Despite your faultless credentials, our new neighbors continued to treat us with caution and suspicion as outsiders, strangers from a different place, carrying with us different customs and different ways. Within the year, they forced us to move on and seek acceptance, or just anonymity, in a small, Basque village. We stayed mainly to ourselves and gave you the benefit of the finest education that our once privileged backgrounds, combined with our meager resources, would allow.

We even made some friends and were beginning to feel, at last, secure, when the Cathar war broke out. Northern knights flattened our fields and scattered our sheep and cried "holy war," in their fervor to purify our village. It did not take them long to expand the definition of the enemy to include me. Fernando decided to go to the captain and swear that we had been married lawfully, in the church, and that you and he were baptized Christians, but I knew that such a move would not stay the captain's bloody hand.

Teresa, you must not try to find us. In the next village, there is a woman named Catarina Balterra. She came to me several times for treatment of her headaches, and we have become friends. Tell her that I beg her to give you shelter, and I pray to God, she may take you in and raise you as her own. Be a good girl and help her as much as you can. Leave everything behind, except the basic necessities. Go, quickly, and may God go with you. You carry with you always your father's love and mine.

Love Always,
Maman

PART ONE
TERESA AND MIQUEL

CHAPTER 1

The black-robed wanderer shook the dust from his sandaled feet before shouldering open the door to the bishop's residence. In his meanderings, he had passed through Lescar before, although he rarely rested long enough to wear out his welcome. He was, after all, a scholar, a priest, and a scientist, meaning that most people considered his ideas strange and his methods downright dangerous.

His long journey had begun in Toledo, in the Kingdom of Castile and Leon. There, he had worked, among other things, on a Latin translation of Aristotle's *Physics*, for his friend and patron. Ugolino Cardinal di Conti, in Ostia, outside of Rome. He took the translation to the Abbey of Fontevraud, where the monks made several fine, illuminated copies. Our wandering scholar took one copy on his return journey, via the southerly Provençal route to Rome. In need of respite, he decided to make a courtesy call on the newly appointed bishop of Lescar, whose town was on the pilgrim way.

Once inside, he spied a large gathering of officials, as well as the simply curious, in the spacious anteroom, where a Church court proceeding was in session. As a widely traveled priest and scholar, he had participated in more than his share of Church trials on both sides of the bench, but he had never come to regard them as part of his priestly or scholarly vocations.

"Who speaks for the accused?" The head of the ecclesiastical tribunal, Monsenhor Raymond III, the new bishop of Lescar, glowered from his throne at the rag-covered, black-haired, olive-complexioned woman seated on the raised floor of the docket before his bench. Her hands and feet were bound in irons, and her coal-black hair was ratty and disheveled. She was clearly frightened, not only of the bishop, but of the four falcon-like clerics seated around him. She both heard and understood him, but she thought it best to mask her fluency in Latin beneath the demure visage of a local woman, more comfortable with the common Langue d'Oc.

The stranger observed the prisoner carefully and concluded that he had seen her before under different and more pleasing circumstances. He had a vague recollection of a woman and a boy for whom he had celebrated the Hispanic liturgy, during his journey from Toledo to Fontevraud, but it was not this formless memory that arrested his attention. He looked past the grit and chains and concentrated, instead, on her extraordinarily large, luminous, chestnut-brown eyes. They spoke to him, and without willing it, he imagined her in an Arab hijab, such as those he had seen in Toledo, with nothing but those arresting eyes visible beneath the veil. Ashamed of his reverie, he quickly brought himself back to the present.

"I speak for the accused," came the voice, in clear, classical Latin, of the thin, black-robed, red-haired man who had just recovered from his daydream about the recently reconquered cities of Islamic Hispania. "Is it asking too much to request that these proceedings be conducted in Occitan rather than Latin so that the accused can understand something of the charges you intend to bring against her?"

"And you are..."

"Oh, I've been known by several names, depending on where I am in my travels. On this side of the Pyrenees, people call me Paire Miquel Escorial. In London, they refer to Father Michael Scot. In Paris, it's Père Michel Écossais. In Bologna, I'm known as Padre Michael lo Scozzese. You may take your pick."

A thin and sour-faced monk, his newly trimmed tonsure shining in the light of the candles by his seat at the prosecutorial table, rose to address the visitor. "Your reputation precedes you, my friend. The texts and translations of Michaelus Scottus concerning philosophy, mathematics, astrology, and alchemy are the subjects of disputation in the greatest universities in Europe! It is rumored that you are a dabbler in magic and sorcery!"

"That's an exaggeration, I assure you," replied the tall man in the black robe. He looked remarkably fit, for a man already in his fifties. "You may consider me a seeker of God's truth, wherever the search may lead me, but I'm also an ordained priest, well versed in Canon Law and qualified to practice before this court."

Bishop Raymond looked bored. The black robed figure, to his right, raised his hand dismissively. "We will stipulate that Pater Michaelus is qualified to represent the accused, in this case."

"And what of my motion for a change in language?" said Paire Miquel, again directing his question to the bishop.

"Denied," came the voice from the bench. "We will proceed in accordance Church law and accepted practices and customs. Fra. Lorenzo will call witnesses whose testimony will direct the result of this inquiry, as God will so determine the decision of the judges."

"But is this court not bound by Church law to first present an *accusatio,* wherein the prisoner profits from the right to confront her accuser? Are we not entitled to hear the charges leveled against the accused and to plead our case?"

"This, Fra Michaelus, is a court of inquiry. We shall hear testimony concerning the accused and judge her accordingly." The bishop's reply was perfunctory and condescending, as if he were chastising a recalcitrant student.

"Priests inquire in order to instruct and enlighten, not to accuse and punish. Our business is saving souls, not burning bodies!" replied the red-haired priest, with no little indignation.

"Who said anything about burning bodies? Besides, sometimes it is necessary to mortify the body in order to save the soul," pronounced the bishop with an officious air.

"Mortification must be both voluntary and moderate, else ineffective and self-indulgent. Besides, if I may be permitted, your Lordship does not give the appearance of a man who has overly mortified himself or denied himself the least physical indulgence or comfort."

"That will be quite enough on that score, learned Father. Should you choose to continue, I am quite content to hold you in contempt, and I certainly do not give you permission to make me the subject of this inquiry," replied the bishop with an irritated wave of his puffy and bejeweled hand.

"I shall refrain, in future, from any such personal observations," said the properly chastised priest.

"That being settled, we shall proceed to the calling of witnesses. Brother Lorenzo, by your leave."

The Cluniac monk with the newly tonsured head and his plain black tunic tied at the waist by a simple chord, rose to his feet, bowed low to the presiding bishop, and intoned in Latin: "Call Pascale Senorant!"

"Pascale Senorant!" parroted the sergeant-at-arms in an unnecessarily loud and commanding voice.

From his seat sprang a rag covered boy, looking at once apprehensive and self-important at being called to give his testimony first. He approached the tribunal, with only a sidelong glance at the chained woman and the red-haired priest at her side. Standing before the Bishop's clerk, he swore his oath, on pain of the loss of his immortal soul, and then faced Fra. Lorenzo to hear and understand the questions which the prosecutor would submit.

"Pascale Senorant, had you several occasions to view the house and dependencies of Madame Balterra, here present?" inquired Fra Lorenzo in a stilted formality commensurate with his status before this court.

The witness, a lad of no more than 10 summers, looked from his interrogator to the bishop, to the red-haired priest and back to Fra Lorenzo. He wore a vague and confused expression that belied the quick intelligence with which Paire Miquel was shortly to credit him. After a long silence, he managed to stammer what sounded like a garbled restatement of the question. "You mean, did I see her ostau (house) and the ort (garden)? Oc (yes). I saw them, but I was not in them, monsenhor."

Fra Lorenzo was at a loss to come up with a valid response. "Did he say sic or non (yes or no)?"

"My lord," Paire Miquel said with a weariness that the whole assembled court was experiencing. "If we engage someone to translate Fra Lorenzo's Latin into a speech that pastoral witnesses might understand and then translate the witness's responses into the proper Latin that my learned colleague is expecting, this procedure may very well last longer than your lordship's appointed length of days! I again respectfully petition your lordship to permit the use of the common tongue, except for the issuance of official documents."

"Very well," the bishop replied without even trying to hide his irritation. "Fra Lorenzo, you will question the boy, and all your future peasant witnesses, in Occitan, but the scribe will record the testimony in proper Latin."

At this, the hapless monk who was acting as court reporter gave a desperate look heavenward and grasped his pen in a vain attempt to convey to it some power and linguistic agility of which he knew he was not in possession.

The boy was visibly relieved when Fra Lorenzo restated his question in the local vernacular. "Oc, I saw the thatch-roofed house and the neat, rectangular gardens that surround it, where she grows her herbs and medicinal plants, and the path that winds through the gardens to the tiny chapel she keeps with her son, Aidor. But I swear I have never been in that house, those gardens, or that chapel myself. I only spied them from my vantage point on the colina (hill) that rises between the sheep path from the village and madame's settlement."

"And what use does the accused make of these herbs and plants?" Lorenzo was anxious to get to the point as quickly as he was able, for there was something about the boy's earnestness that made him uneasy.

"Oh, I'm sure I don't know, your worshipfulness," said the boy, his eyes animated and wandering. "All I know is that when people would journey from the village to see her and sit for refreshments on her porch, she would immediately go to one of her gardens and pick some leaves, stalks, or flowers with the utmost care and take them into her house, from which she would come out some ten minutes later with a small beaker or bottle in her hand. Her guest would express pleasure upon receiving it and offer madame a few tasty morsels in return. They would chat and eat and sip their concoctions and eventually relax enough to unburden themselves of whatever might be troubling them. Madame always had time for her visitors, all the time in the world, to sit and drink, to wander inside or to stroll the gardens, or just to listen. Folks always left more peaceful and certainly smiling more than when they had arrived."

"What was in those relaxing concoctions that Madame served?" Fra Lorenzo looked interested and encouraging.

"Oh, I wouldn't know, your lordship. I'm only a lad, and I'm never permitted to snack with the grown-ups!"

"But what do people say it is?" pursued the prosecutor, moving closer to the trembling child.

"My lord," the red-haired priest interrupted with both indignation and impatience in his voice. "My learned colleague calls for the witness to speculate about a matter with which he could not have first-hand knowledge!"

"Surely, my lord, the witness can tell us truthfully the substance of the village gossip about this crucial piece of evidence," the prosecutor replied with rodent-like petulance.

"Village swains may listen to gossip at roadside taverns to amuse themselves, but this is a court of LAW, and would be best advised to take note only of evidence arrived at through direct experience!" Paire Miquel resumed his seat without trying to hide his disgust.

"I trust, Fra Lorenzo, that we will hear testimony from witnesses who have actually tasted these concoctions," answered the learned bishop from his elevated chair, "in which case we will await this testimony before trusting our ears to whatever the boy may have heard."

Thus chastised, the prosecutor moved to another line of questioning. "Young Senorant, did you ever see madame take anyone into her tiny chapel?"

"Never," said the boy, "except for her son and for Paire Miquel over there at madame's side.

"You are referring to Pater Michaelus Scottus over there?"

"Oc," said the boy, looking as if he had inadvertently said something he shouldn't have.

Paire Miquel rose once again to his feet. "My lord, I am perfectly prepared to tell this court precisely what I said, what I did, and what I saw, but I will not have you treat as evidence anything that comes from the mouth of this boy, who observed all of this from a distant hillside!"

The bishop indulgently smiled at the red-headed priest and reassured him that the court was not at all interested in information about him. On the other hand, it would vigorously seek out any information that would shed light on madame's actions and motivation, concerning this sleepy village.

"And you foresee that this BOY can afford us some useful insights into complex adult motivations?"

The bishop frowned, thinking how he might deliver a pithy response. Finally, he abandoned the effort. "We seek facts, only facts," he said, making no attempt to hide his annoyance. "This court will make its own inferences from the testimony given."

"In accordance with the LAW," added Paire Miquel, as if to complete the bishop's thought.

"Of course, of course," admitted the bishop, in no mood to grant the defense the final word.

"Well then," continued Fra Lorenzo, as if the interruption had not occurred, "what did you see when you viewed the house of Mme. Balterra from your vantage point on the hillside?"

"Just the house, the veranda, the gardens, and the chapel."

"And what artifacts were there in this mysterious chapel, young man?" The prosecutor moved ever closer to the witness, as if to block his view of anyone else in the courtroom.

"Again, I call the court's attention to the fact that young Pascale could not have seen inside the chapel from his perch on the hillock, unless he subsequently paid a visit to the property, a visit to which he has not testified!" Paire Miquel had once again risen to his feet and was instructing the court as a teacher might draw a reluctant student's attention to some self-evident truth.

"Was there a cross on top of the chapel?" asked Fra Lorenzo, not even affording the bishop enough time to respond to the objection.

"Non, your worship, nothing that I could make out from where I was lying." The boy was confused but perfectly prepared to be truthful.

"And did Mme. Balterra's guests go into this structure? Were they invited to do so?"

"Non. I never saw any of madame's guests enter the chapel. No one except her film (son)…and Paire Miquel," the boy answered with a furtive glance in the direction of the defense table.

"Very well," said Fra Lorenzo, looking meaningfully first at Paire Miquel and then at the bishop. Then, as if changing his mind about something he was about to say, he turned once again toward Pascale Senorant and asked him in a gentle voice, "And who was Mme. Balterra's visitor that day?"

"Madame Barroux, the cabinetmaker's wife, a very important lady in the village." The boy's eyes expressed surprise that Fra Lorenzo would ask a question the answer to which he already knew.

"Then I call Madame Clotilde Barroux to the witness stand," the prosecutor pronounced with a confident smirk on his face.

"Point of order, Monseigneur Bishop," Paire Miquel interrupted with no little annoyance. "Have I not the right to ask the witness some questions of my own?"

"Proceed, Father, if your intent is to elucidate the matter rather than to create further confusion."

"As it may please your excellencies," began the red-headed priest, rising to his feet in a more unhurried manner. Turning to the boy, who would no doubt have preferred to leave the witness stand, Paire Miquel spoke softly, slowing down his delivery considerably and interspersing as many old Occitan words as he thought he could get away with in front of the bishop. "How many times would you say that you spied on Mme. Balterra from your favorite hillside perch?"

"Oh, I don't know. Perhaps three or four times a week? Most of the time, I was just trying to find out when I could see Aidor—that's Mme. Balterra's son, you know—alone, by himself, walking in the hills, so I could be friends with him and play with him."

"I see," said Paire Miquel thoughtfully. "Then, in all these times, you must have seen many people coming and going from Mme. Balterra's."

"Oc, I have! Why, there's Madame Barroux, Monsieur Fenin, the tin smith, Mademoiselle Cortier, from the Delisse Bakery Shop, Paul Mortais, the postman, Curé Antoine—"

"That will be enough," said the bishop as if to stop the boy from reciting the names of the whole village. "Father Michaelus, what is your point with respect to this recitation of names?"

"Only that a great many people visit Mme. Balterra on a regular basis, and yet my learned colleague sees fit only to call on those who have not experienced complete satisfaction with what they have received from her, to give witness here against her."

"Very well, Father, we give you leave to call whomever you choose, as long as they have something relevant to say, and as long as you submit the list to me and to Fra Lorenzo for prior approval."

"And on what grounds do you intend to give or withhold that approval, my lord?" Father Miquel was careful to restrain his argumentative tone of voice.

"On the grounds of relevancy and in the interest of justice," replied the bishop with all the dignity he could muster.

"Very well," said the red-haired priest before turning back to the witness and posing a final question, almost as an afterthought. "Tell us, Pascale, did you ever get the opportunity to play with Mme. Balterra's son, Aidor?"

"Oh, oc, I did. We were the best of friends. Aidor is really a fine fellow, except for his funny accent. He's kind and good and generous…"

"A good, Christian boy, would you say?" Father Miquel added with a sly smile directed toward the presiding tribunal. Fra Lorenzo rose rapidly to his feet in a show of indignation and outrage.

"Does Pater Michaelus intend us to take the testimony of this child as to what constitutes a good Christian?"

"Precisely my point, my lord. I have no further questions of this witness," the red-headed priest replied with a wave of his hand.

Fra Lorenzo looked as if he had been hit on the back of the head by a pebble. Refusing to make visible his evident embarrassment, he shuffled the papers in front of him and made to call Mme. Barroux, the witness he had attempted to call ten minutes ago. The bishop, however, who had been squirming uncomfortably in his seat, interrupted him long enough to say that the testimony they had heard today had been quite enough for one sitting and that the court had determined to adjourn itself until after Matins the next morning.

All rose out of respect for the bishop, and after he had left the dais, they began filing out of the meeting room.

CHAPTER 2

Father Miquel followed the gaolers who were bringing Mme. Balterra back to her prison cell, and he asked to be admitted to consult with her. The head gaoler reluctantly gave him leave and, seeing that the chained woman was in no position or state of health to inflict any harm, left them to their consultation.

The red-haired priest, still trying to ascertain where he had seen her last, inquired as to her state of health and nourishment, producing an apple and a hard crust of bread from the sleeves of his black robe without even waiting for an answer. He sat next to her on the hard wooden bench that was the only furniture in the tiny cell besides the bedroll and the chamber pot. He pulled a waterskin from the folds of his gown and offered her a drink of the, by now, warm but clean liquid inside. Gradually she began to breathe normally.

Father Miquel waited patiently until the thirty-some-year-old lady stopped shaking and fixed her frightened gaze on his concerned face. He smiled at her (probably the first to do so today) and asked her where her parents were from.

"They were both from Toledo, when it was still part of what we used to call Al-Andalus, of the Taifa of Seville, but I am NOT a Saracen or Berber. I was raised a Christian, a traditional Hispania Christian. There were many of us in Toledo.

"When the Christian kings of the north took the city back, they preserved the old ties between Christians, Jews and Muslims, even encouraged our wise men to work together to translate the old books from Greek and Arabic into Latin. But the more God seemed to favor the Christians, the more Christian kings learned to use religious ties as a measure of future loyalty. They even began to suspect their fellow

Christians of disloyalty, if they clung to the old rites and kept the old texts in Arabic characters. As you well know, I have one such book, beautifully hand-painted by one of the artisan scribes whom both the Jews and Arabs also employed to make copies of their holy books. It is a treasure that I shall always keep safe from ignorant hands!"

Father Miquel looked interested in the subject of the book, but he made a note to himself and put that question aside for the time being. "And how did you end up in Bastanès? It's really something of a backwater compared to a place like Toledo."

"Well, things just began to change too rapidly for my family. My father was a very learned man who used to teach mathematics and astronomy at the Islamic University of Cordoba. He worked with famous scientists and astrologers from Bagdad, Milan, Cologne, and all over the world, but then he made a fateful choice, one which would change our lives forever.

"One of his distinguished colleagues was a Jewish scholar named Moishe Ben Elizer, at whose home my father used to spend countless hours discussing philosophy and the fascinating study of numerology, of which Ben Elizer was the world's expert."

"I knew Ben Elizer," said Father Miquel. "He and I worked on a numerical sequencing problem that both of us had first encountered in Tuscany, from the mathematician Leonardo da Pisa."

"Now, in addition to a brilliant mind, Ben Elizer also had a beautiful daughter, upon whom he doted and determined to bestow the finest education of which ANYONE in Toledo would have been envious."

A startled expression broke out on Father Miquel's face. "That's where I've seen those eyes before. She has her mother's eyes," Father Miquel thought to himself

The woman ignored his change of expression. "As she was clearly capable of leaving the wisest of men speechless when it came to the subtleties of Greek and Arabic philosophy, Ben Elizer included her in the lively discussions with my father. Little by little, my father realized that he had fallen hopelessly for the beautiful, intelligent, and educated girl who was to become my mother.

"It was their decision to marry that was to drive a wedge between my father and the newly victorious northerners who held the upper hand in the delicate racial and religious balance that was Toledo after the Christian kings began seizing more territory. Not that Ben Elizer had anything against my father. On the contrary, he loved him like a son, but the new Christian conquerors of the north were suspicious of the good relations that had been cultivated over the centuries between our communities.

"The old Christians had taken to wearing Arab dress and speaking Arabic in the marketplaces, even though they spoke their own patois among themselves. Their scholars had even produced sacred Christian texts in their own simple Latin, represented in Arabic characters, all part of their outward conformity to the old Islamic regimes. When the conquerors arrived, they found three powerful communities, each with its own cherished beliefs and traditions but with a long history of interaction and cooperation, especially in the academic pursuits."

"And what precipitated this conflict?" inquired the priest, masking his knowledge of the friction which had already begun to alter Toledo, while he was still working there.

"The authorities waited until my father had gone to the priest and secured their marriage and a promise from my mother that she would raise any children in the Christian faith. Then the priests summoned Toledo's head rabbi and told him of the union, hoping to incite the Hispanic Christians against the Jewish community."

"I take it they succeeded," said Paire Miquel, his head moving closer to that of the prisoner.

"Indeed, they did," replied Mme. Balterra, her eyes darting up to his in her anxiety to convey the urgency of the situation. "The northern Christians took advantage of the controversy to launch a major persecution of Jews and Muslims. They burned down homes, mosques, and synagogues. They burned down libraries and private collections to purify their city of all godless knowledge. They even rounded up Christians who wore Arabic clothing and conducted their liturgies in the traditional Hispanic manner."

"My parents were forced to flee Toledo, along with my grandfather, but his separation from his treasured book collection and the faith of his fathers was too much for him. He died along the way, on the outskirts of some dusty shepherd's village hidden away in the base of the Spanish Pyrenees.

"My parents wandered from one village to the next, carefully guarding their identities. It was during these travels and brief, transient sojourns that my mother gave birth to me and had me baptized in some little village church."

Without interrupting Mme. Balterra's story, Father Miquel scribbled a note to himself.

"They didn't even know when they had left Spain, one Basque-speaking village being much like another, until they began meeting northern merchants who could still communicate with the locals, mixing in more frequently with local market days."

"And that's how you ended up here," concluded the priest, his mind retracing the waywardness of his own journey, back from the multicultural center of Toledo, as it had been when he had last seen it.

Mme. Balterra looked tired after her ordeal, which had started so early that day and seemed destined to never end. Father Michael pulled out the last crust of bread that he had been saving for his own repast this evening. Offering the bread to Mme. Balterra, he smiled and backed out of the narrow cell.

Bishop Raymond had offered Father Miquel a list of prospective witnesses, which the priest had stuffed behind the rope encircling his waist like a belt. He made a mental note to cultivate the acquaintance of each of these "witnesses" to learn as much as he could about his client's standing in the community and the kinds of ideas her neighbors harbored about her. In the meantime, he would get some rest and try to digest what he already knew.

•   •   •

Father Miquel lay in his narrow bed in the tiny monastic cell he had been given as temporary lodging near the village. He was experiencing the same sense of bewilderment he supposed most people feel when they return to the old neighborhood, the one that they think will never change, and find everything different. Toledo was like that. In its heyday, it had been a shining center of culture and learning. There were treasures, gold and silver, exotic plants and vines, and knowledge, volumes and volumes of scrolls in Arabic, Hebrew, and Greek, books that reached back centuries into the learned memory of man and distilled the wisdom of countless generations.

Father Miquel had studied and worked there, a friend to monks, rabbis, and mullahs, a seeker of truth in an oasis of knowledge. Now, apparently, the golden age was gone, burned, leveled, irreparably consigned to the past, perhaps to be forgotten in the breathless march of history. While in another part of the world, mindless men at arms, Christian and Muslim, had fought and killed one another in a hopeless mission to recapture the land they both held sacred, scholars of three great traditions had banned together in Toledo to capture and preserve the greater part of their common heritage for generations yet unborn. Now, in the fever of victory, all of this had fallen into ruin in the name of a singular ideology. Never mind that this was Father Miquel's ideology and fundamental belief. Its hegemony had evidently been purchased at a ridiculously high price from the coffers of mankind. What was left? Only ignorance and fear of the unknown. Yet perhaps there was the tiniest spark of guarded knowledge that a few were called upon to nurture and fan into a new and unquenchable fire!

Madame Teresa Balterra was part of that residual spark, and he, Miquel, would not permit that spark to be snuffed out, or so he had convinced himself that his motives were pure and strictly academic. He assured himself that the lingering image of Teresa Balterra's eyes was totally subservient to his scholarly interest in the case. Feeling thus certain of his mission, and having prayed to his Lord for guidance, Paire Miquel fell into a deep and peaceful sleep.

CHAPTER 3

Paire Miquel[1] spent the next morning pleading his case for a continuance, one long enough for him to interview witnesses in the case. Had it not been for the long-established schedule the bishop had put in place months before to receive his episcopal colleague from Toulouse, he would most certainly not have so readily agreed to Paire Miquel's request. Nevertheless, much to Paire Miquel's surprise, he did grant him the entire weekend to prepare his case. Elated with the result, Miquel immediately set out to interview the villagers of Bastanès.

His first meeting was with Mme. Colette Barroux at her home above the cabinetmaker's shop.

"Of course, I knew Mme. Balterra, and I used to visit her house from time to time, but you don't expect me to announce that to all my neighbors, do you? I have my husband's position in the quartier to think of. Consider what people would say, about being associated with a woman so strange, so different, so foreign, with her strange accent and her strange clothes and her strange ways. People say she is a gypsy, or a Jewess, or a Saracen.

"And who do you say she is, based on your numerous meetings with her?" asked the priest.

"I don't know, but she knows more about healing herbs and mushrooms and poultices than even the monks of St. Alban's."

"And you made use of her medicinal knowledge in what way?" pursued the priest.

---

1 Paire is the Occitan spelling of "père," meaning: "father." Miquel is Occitan for Michael.

"I have a persistent rash, here where the collar of my blouse touches my neck. Mme. Balterra prepares a tincture of pomegranate leaves to ease the itching and reduce the swelling. It always makes me feel more comfortable, you know, but the rash comes back, especially in the summertime, when I'm working in the garden." Mme. Barroux smiled pleasantly and offered her guest a cup of tea.

Father Miquel thought for a minute. "Is it an expensive medication?"

"Oh no!" she responded, "We have a kind of barter system. I bring her a pot a savory stew, and she gives me the medication. I make enough for both Teresa and her son."

"You refer to her by her Christian name."

"If she is a Christian," remarked Mme. Barroux, a look of suspicion creeping over her face. "My Gilles saw her also, I found out. She gave him spearmint for his headaches. So he says, but I have my doubts. Maybe she used another remedy for curing his supposed 'headaches.' You never know, but ever since then, I've been leery of her. There's something not right going on here, I'll tell you, she and her son living apart like that. There's something exotic about her that women don't like finding their menfolk around. It's just not healthy, I tell you."

Mme. Barroux's expression became very distant and smug, as if she were remembering something particularly unpleasant. Paire Miquel decided he would get no more out of her on the subject of Teresa Balterra, so he took his leave and turned down the dusty path in the direction of the village bakery shop (both patisserie and boulangerie), a place of gathering and gossip in that tiny community.

Only slightly wider than a goat path, the winding dirt road that passed for the village's central street led from the ramshackle market stalls on the outer edges of the circle to the squat and sleeping Romanesque church at its center. Paire Miquel's walk took him past the blacksmith's shop, a squat cottage with a huge firepit and bellows to one side. From the oversized bellows hung a rope for forcing the diaphragm to close and push a column of air into the hungry mouth of the fire. With a pair of tongs, the smithy lifted a red-hot horseshoe from the fire and held it fast to the anvil. He pounded the horseshoe into shape with his hammer and then submerged it in a bucket of water. Paire Miquel noted the high-pitched sizzle with which the liquid greeted the hot metal.

Across the street from the blacksmith's shop was a store that advertised all sorts of concession items, such as slabs of bacon and sacks of potatoes and all sorts of freshly harvested vegetables, collected and sold for the local farmers. There were sacks of wheat, barley, and finely milled flour from the cooperative mill, which collected everyone's contribution and performed the distribution.

Past the concession store, situated between it and the mill, Paire Miquel found the bakery, its window filled with confections of every shape and variety. The women of the village patronized the fragrant premises twice daily: first, after the ringing of Lauds, to purchase the bread and pastries required for their petit déjeuner (breakfast), and secondly, after nones, in preparation for afternoon repast. At those hours, the shop was alive with the bustle of purchases and the exchange of recently acquired information. Since Paire Miquel's arrival was between these times, the pastry shop was much less crowded and noticeably quieter.

The red-haired priest looked around and spotted a girl of no more than seventeen years endeavoring to look busy for her supervisor's benefit, notwithstanding the lull in business. This, Paire Miquel assumed, was the object of his visit. The priest approached her and addressed her directly.

"Loïsa?" he asked, knowing, already the answer.

"Oc," she replied, looking pleased that he had addressed her. "I am called Loïsa."

"Are you acquainted with Mme. Teresa Balterra?" he asked without any preliminary small talk.

"I visited the herb lady on several occasions to consult on—private matters."

"Loïsa, a woman's freedom and reputation depend on what I can learn to defend her. Tell me, what kind of help were you seeking from Mme. Balterra?"

"There was a boy, the cabinetmaker's apprentice, whom I fancied. He didn't have time for me, and I asked Mme. Teresa for a potion to give him—to stimulate his interest in me."

"A love potion!" said Pair Miquel, a little disappointed with the answer provided.

The salesgirl interrupted her story by serving the red-haired priest a weak beer with parsley in it. Then she returned to the subject at hand, the love potion. "The concoction, Mme. Balterra said, would make him more amicably disposed. Well, it was supposed to, anyway. One day, I brought a cup of it to his shop, and I guess that it worked."

"What do you mean, you *guess*?"

"The next day, he proposed to the blacksmith's daughter, and today they have a strapping son to bless their union, so I suppose it did work—on her."

"And how do you feel about this," said the priest, mildly amused at the unfortunate turn of events.

"I hate her, that ugly witch! May her hair all fall out and her Basque nose sprout a monstrous black wart!"

"Now, now," said the priest, in an effort to calm the young lady down. "You don't suppose that Mme. Balterra had any idea which way his disposition would turn?"

"I don't rightly know, but it seems to me that if someone has that kind of power, they had well better know how to use it!"

"Perhaps so," agreed the priest, "but did Mme. Belterra ever lead you to suspect that she harbored any ill feelings toward you?"

"No, not at all. Quite the opposite, she always welcomed me with a genuine smile and listened to me with patience and compassion. You know what I think, Paire? I think that some unseen evil force used whatever Mme. Teresa did and twisted it around to accomplish its own purposes!"

"I wouldn't be too quick to attribute affairs of the heart to the evil one!" said the priest, flashing her a quick smile. "I would wager that he has weightier things with which to concern himself."

"Well, that's what he told me, he did. Standin' right where you are, he looked seriously at me and told me it was the work of the devil to twist around people's intensions and make it all come out the wrong way!"

"Who told you this?" demanded Paire Miquel, his brow furrowed in sudden interest.

"Why, Brother Lorenzo, of course, when he was in here gathering information for the bishop's inquiry. He said the devil has all kinds of ways to cause us difficulty and discomfort!"

"Well, I wouldn't be too sure that Brother Lorenzo knows any more about what the devil wants than you or I. Did he suggest that anyone might have assisted the devil in bringing about his mischief?"

"Oc. He said that most times, people act as the devil's helpers and that he rewards them by giving them special powers."

"Powers and skills such as Mme. Balterra possesses?"

"Aye, he said that, and I can surely believe it!"

"And Brother Lorenzo suggested that you might believe all this?"

"Well, he sort of brought it all together for me, but I've been able to see it myself for some time!"

"I see," said the priest, although there were many arguments he could have offered to counter Brother Lorenzo's assertions. "And do you have a young man in whom you are interested now?"

"Oh, oc, I am engaged to the eldest son of the tinsmith, Sendat. He is very handsome and very rich, and I am quite fortunate to have made such a match!"

"Such good fortune must come from God and not the devil, you might say," Paire Miquel added with a slight smile.

"Assuredly," agreed the girl, failing to follow the priest's line of reasoning. The young girl had a far-away look in her eyes, as if she were mentally comparing these two young men and wondering what life might have been like if things had gone differently.

With that, Paire Miquel took his leave and retraced his steps to the blacksmith's hut.

CHAPTER 4

At the ringing of Sext, the apprentices and journeymen took their lunch, and the forge, without the continual stoking provided by its tenders, slowly began to cool. When Paire Miquel arrived, the blacksmith, Jacques Malin, was sitting on a wooden bench next to his still-red-hot forge, enjoying the fresh air without the bustle and noise of the day's work. Paire Miquel waved a greeting, and the burley tradesman beckoned to his visitor to come and partake in a cup of wine.

He barked a peremptory order into the open door, and a thin and disheveled woman emerged holding a still-corked bottle in her shaking hand and looking genuinely frightened at the prospect of interacting with the master of the house. There was a red and blue spot under one of her eyes, and her lower lip was protruding and swollen.

"How do you expect our guest to drink when the bottle is still corked?" The woman scurried inside to find the tire bouchon (bottle opener) and to remove herself from the master's sight. She emerged with an open bottle and a fresh glass.

"Well, don't just stand there like a blithering idiot! Pour the wine for our guest and thank him for his visit!"

The woman stammered a welcome, intentionally avoiding eye contact with the priest, and then she permitted herself a single, furtive, pleading glance before once again averting her eyes and disappearing into the house.

Paire Miquel hastened to present himself, explaining his role as Mme. Balterra's counsel and the purpose of his visit. The blacksmith immediately twisted his face in irritation and seized his wine bottle in token of a sudden decision not to share an additional drop. His bloodshot pale-gray eyes were hostile, and his attitude was that of a man who would fight with the priest were he not afraid to do so.

"Damned gitan (gypsy) witch!" exploded the tradesman, his hand forming the huge fist that he used to intimidate those who had the temerity to challenge him. "You tell her to keep her foreign nose out of my family's affairs or she'll find herself on the receiving end of my fist, she will."

"I advise against striking a woman with those enormous hands of yours, but what precisely did she do to your family?"

"Never you mind! It's none of your business. No, and none of hers, either! And you can tell her I said so, you can." The angry craftsman got up and stomped into the house without the slightest attempt at civility, slamming the cottage door behind him.

Paire Miquel made a mental note to have a meeting with Mme. Malin when he saw a chance to be alone with her someday, but for now, he considered his interview over.

He was on his way back to the sheep path when he spotted one of Malin's apprentices getting up from under a large weeping birch on the other side of the path and sauntering over to meet him. The youth couldn't help overhearing what Malin had said to the priest, so loud and obnoxious he had become, and he evidently had something to say about it. The priest could see that the young man was smiling and, no doubt, braver than he would have been if the blacksmith were still out of doors. As the young man approached the priest, he gave him a knowing smile.

"I suppose you've gotten an earful from old man Malin just now, haven't you?"

"Yes, I suppose I have," replied Paire Miquel, looking a little flustered by the experience.

The young apprentice, encouraged by the priest's lack of complete composure, took a seat on a nearby tree stump and decided to bring his listener up to date,

"Old man Malin is a singularly unpleasant fellow, especially to those who are shorter and weaker than he is."

"Like his young apprentices?" asked the priest.

"Oc, I've got the scars on my back to prove it…as do his wife, daughter, and the neighborhood children, anyone except his giant of a journeyman, Pierre, who gets to do or not do whatever he wants around here."

"You mean, M. Malin cannot control Pierre?"

"No, he's totally frustrated by him, and he takes out his frustration on the rest of us."

"Including his wife and daughter?"

"Especially them, but first, he's got to get himself good and drunk!"

Worry lines distorted Paire Miquel's face. "And then he beats them?"

"One of them, anyway. Margot, his daughter, made her escape last year by getting married to the cabinetmaker's son. I hear that strange lady, the dark-haired foreigner that nobody admits to talking to, had somethin' to do with it."

Paire Miquel's face registered surprise and interest. "Have *you* ever met this foreigner?"

"Not I, no. I'm sure the master would beat me senseless if he suspected I had!"

"But Margot is all right now?"

"Aye, she's doing well, and her little one is getting bigger every day!"

At that moment, Malin emerged from the squat and vine-entangled cottage, a tankard of ale in his hand. Immediately he caught sight of his young apprentice and the red-haired priest, who was evidently still sneaking around his shop. Malin's face reddened with anger as he dropped his mug to the ground and scooped up a stick from the entranceway. Then he charged toward the man and boy, who were still deep in conversation, and began growling at the boy, uncontrolled spittle dripping from his lips.

"Esteve, you little mound of steaming goat shit, what are you telling that meddlesome priest? I'll teach you to share our secrets with strangers!"

Having closed the distance between himself and the youth, the blacksmith raised his flexible stick to come down, whip-like, on the back, shoulders, and arms of the defenseless boy.

Midway through his swing, however, the priest's massive hand met his wrist. Paire Miquel's black robe slipped down, revealing the sinews of an arm not unaccustomed to either arduous work or self-defense. For a long moment, the two arms were suspended in mid-air, neither able to overcome the other, and then Malin showed the slightest look of fear and doubt on his face. He released the stick and lowered his hand.

The priest's face reflected the anger he felt at having been compelled to resort to force. He looked at Malin with such an unaccustomed level of disgust that he even surprised himself. He glared at the blacksmith and said in a low, throaty voice, "I'm giving you fair warning about seeking ANY reprisals against this boy. I'm putting him under the protection of Pierre, and your wife, as well. If you should raise your hand to either of them, or to Margot, Pierre will provide the appropriate lesson till you see fit to change your behavior. Do you understand me?"

"I do," said the chastised blacksmith, looking both resentful and shamefaced, at the same time.

Paire Miquel turned to the apprentice, who had been spared a whipping. "Esteve," said the priest, "what is your nom de famille (family name)?"

"D'Abbadie," said the boy, with some misgivings as to why the priest required this information.

"I probably won't need to call on you, but just in case I need to discredit a prosecution witness, I'll thank you for your honesty in coming up to me today."

Malin had already slunk away, so he had not overheard the previous exchange.

"Will you really tell Pierre to protect us?" the boy asked with some trepidation in his voice.

"No," replied the priest, "but Malin will think I have, and he'll leave you alone. You needn't worry about him anymore."

"Thank you, Paire," the boy said before scurrying back to his work.

CHAPTER 5

Vespers with the monks was a welcome relief from Paire Miquel's journey to the disappointing side of human nature. The left aisle of the choir chanted the antiphon:

Auxilium nostrum in nomine Domini.　　　Our help is in the name of the Lord.

To which the right aisle responded:

Qui fecit coelum et terram.　　　Who made heaven and earth.

What perfect symmetry; what balance and proportionality there are in singing! Nature itself craves and builds such structure and beauty. This thirst for harmony and balance is the basis of our painting, our architecture, our sculpture, and our science. There is no light without shadow, height without depth, rejoicing without sorrow, life without death. Paire Miquel reflected upon the irony to be found in mankind's inability to live as it prays, sings, and builds!

Paire Miquel's mind wandered to his treasured Aristotelian manuscript and to a quiet street in Rome, now so many years ago, when he was first struck with the idea of an experiment with the nature of light. He rushed back to his rooms on the grounds of the Monasterio Santi Quattro Coronati, with its view of the San Giovanni Laterano. He begged the abbot to let him construct on the grounds, where he walled in a dark room with a small aperture to let in the light of day. In the path of the beam of light, he positioned a polished shard of glass through which the light filtered, turning it into all the colors of the rainbow. How neat and symmetrical were the bands of color, from red to violet, stretching out into the darkened room! How structured and organic is the working of light and colors hidden within it!

His only mistake was that, in his enthusiasm, he showed his work to the monks at Santi Quattro Coronati and other curiosity seekers in that great city. His method of scientific inquiry through experimentation was viewed with some degree of skepticism, and those who witnessed the separation of light into colors were quick to accuse the red-headed scholar of magic and sorcery. It was uncanny how otherwise intelligent people, when faced with something new and unexplained, resort to the occult to account for it! Many, of course, knew that it was a perfectly natural phenomenon, but some refused even to listen to an explanation. Fortunately, he enjoyed the unqualified admiration and protection of Pope Honorius III, who, as the younger Cercio Savelli, had been his teacher at the University of Boulogne, so no one dared touch him. Nevertheless, Paire Miquel knew that there were those who did not wish him well.

Once vespers were concluded, Paire Miquel made his way to his cell to consider how they might proceed with the case of Mme. Belterra.

So, people do not profess to know or visit Teresa by day, but they visit her secretly and use her gifts to their advantage. And she likes to help people who shun her in public, especially the weak and the vulnerable! What an extraordinary woman to wear the badge of a foreigner and an outcast, and yet to be so forgiving of the people who shun her! How is it that people are so naturally suspicious of anyone who comes from a different place and works using a separate set of beliefs and assumptions? But in the case of Mme. Balterra, people can't seem to agree even about what that set of traditions and system of beliefs may have been. He resolved to speak with her again and to allow himself some additional probing into her background and character.

Paire Miquel raided the monk's pantry to fill a sack with some bread, a couple of pieces of fruit, and a wedge of hard cheese. He then set off to his client's prison cell. The sun was just peeking above the hills when the gaoler checked the priest's sack for any knives, axes, or other contraband before ushering him into Mme. Balterra's damp pit.

Teresa was grateful for the additions to her diet of thin gruel, and she seemed less tense and anxious than she had been the other day, directly after her encounter with the court of inquiry. The priest gave her some water and hoped that she would find it easier to talk freely with him.

"My earliest memories as a little girl are of journeys, endless journeys, with my mother and father, up and down countless hills, for miles and miles over dusty, stony sheep paths. I remember my father carrying his books till his back was permanently bent in two and my mother telling stories about Toledo, its palaces, libraries, and gardens. She would dwell upon the gardens, describing each and every tree, flower, and herb. Mother would describe the shape of every stem, leaf, and flower. She would tell me how they should be prepared, and which combinations were effective for treating particular illnesses or producing desired effects. I could close my eyes and see those plants as plainly as I see your face, but we never stayed in one place long enough to cultivate them. Always, we were forced to move on because one person or another would denounce my mother as a Jewess or my father as a gypsy. I swore that one day, when I had a home of my own, I would plant gardens of flowering plants and herbs. Then I would help people as my mother always did.

"My father had me baptized because he believed, as I now do, in Jesus, our Lord. But my mother's curse, I still carry with me. When I was ten, Mother and Father were both murdered by fanatics, leaving me alone in the world.

"The Balterras took me in, though I was too numb to acknowledge their goodness. We lived in their Basque village until I was seventeen and their son, Aidor, asked his father, my guardian, for my hand in marriage.

"At last, my life as a nomad and a wanderer would come to an end. With Aidor at my side, I would have a home of my own; I would be part of a community that knew who I was, cared about me, and would protect me from whatever might happen. We had a son, whom we named Aidor, after his father, and I was sure that unlike his mother, he would grow up in one place.

"Then the second war came, the crusade against the Cathars, which swept through our village like a plague. Neighbor turned on neighbor, and everyone's loyalties and religious orthodoxy were put in question. There I was, the foreigner, the daughter of a Jewish mother, a natural target for people looking for someone to punish. Besides, the frightened parish priest, under torture, admitted to the invaders that we had a Dominican friar who celebrated the Mass for us using the old Hispanic rite instead of the Roman liturgy. That was enough to put us under suspicion of heresy.

"Nevertheless, my husband went to the knight, the northerner who had taken over our village. Big Aidor insisted we were good Christians and should be protected. The knight's dagger responded for him. Our house was burned to the ground. All that I was able to salvage of my father's scholarly past in Toledo was a single book, my book in Arabic characters that I keep with me always. My husband was murdered, and I was desperate, with no idea what to do or where to go."

Again, she spoke of the book! He made a mental note to pursue that thread, but for now, he was loath to interrupt her.

"Fortunately, the band of friars who helped us maintain our accustomed worship according to the Hispanic liturgy offered sanctuary for my son and me in the thatched hut that served as their friary. Under cover of darkness, we escaped, disguised as wandering mendicants, and took, once again, to the hills as homeless wanderers.

"Once peace had been restored, we ventured into the little hamlet of Bastanès. There were many abandoned farmhouses in those days, in the aftermath of war, and little Aidor and I took possession of one on the outskirts of town. We told people nothing about us, giving them, we hoped, no reason to persecute us. I was determined that we should become self-sufficient, growing our own food and keeping our own chickens and farm animals."

"Did you attend the parish church?" inquired the priest.

"No," answered Teresa. "I wanted our isolation to be complete. Some missionary friars passed our village every couple of months, and they would say Mass for us in our little chapel in the old Hispanic way. No, our isolation was complete, except that I also had my herb gardens, where I cultivated the healing remedies my mother had told me about. Little by little, people began to visit us, having heard rumors of the remedies I could offer. I gave them herbal tea and a sympathetic ear, and gradually they felt inclined to confide in me."

"Otherwise, they kept as far from you as you kept from them?" inquired Paire Miquel, trying to interrupt her story as little as possible.

"That's true. We developed a kind of understanding that in the village, should we happen to pass one another, we would pretend not to be aware of each other, but when they came privately to the house, we would share tea and confidences."

"And has this worked, by and large, to define your relationship with your neighbors?" Paire Miquel thought about the attitudes he had witnessed in the village.

"Not completely. There are people who remained suspicious of me, and there are those who have developed an outright animosity where Aidor and I are concerned. And for my son, this isolation has been particularly difficult. He needs someone else in his life besides his mother. A boy needs friends and companions to play with. I shall never forgive myself for depriving my son of this. Not that I can see another option for us!"

"What other enterprises have your neighbors' confidences opened up for you?" asked the red-haired priest.

"My skills as a midwife have been sought out by a number of the young women in the village—a service I have been happy to accept."

Mme. Balterra shifted her position only slightly, but with an expression of excruciating pain on her face. Paire Miquel looked down and saw the bloody open sores that the chain cuffs had left on the woman's wrists and ankles. Horrified, he reached down to touch them, but with increasing agony, the woman moved away from his grip.

"There must be something I can do!" said the priest. He pulled a cloth from his cassock and offered to clean the fresh blood.

"Find my son, my Aidor, and go with him to our farmhouse. He'll take you into the herb garden, where you'll find some dill. Aidor will show you how to pulverize it and mix it with very little alcohol. That would help me immeasurably… You know that it's not magic?"

"Of course, I do!" the priest said without hesitation. "But first I need to make another visit."

Paire Miquel stooped through the narrow door of Mme. Balterra's cell and made straight for the bishop's residence in the center of town. The bishop's guest had left that morning, and Bishop Raymond seemed relieved not to be in the presence of someone who might be judgmental of his comportment.

Once escorted into the bishop's study, Paire Miquel bowed and reached for the bishop's hand to kiss his ring. The bishop, however, had had his fill of formal interviews.

"Please, please, no ceremony, Pater Michaelus. It's refreshing to be with someone for whom I don't have to perform! What brings you here a full day before the resumption of the hearing?"

"You'll pardon the interruption, my lord, but I come to you on a matter of some urgency."

"Please, speak freely, Michaelus. We're not in public court!"

"My lord, since you have given me permission to speak frankly, it concerns Mme. Balterra. She's in terrible pain due to the cuts from her shackles. I fear the open wounds will cause swelling and gangrene!"

"And you wish me to relieve her of these shackles? You know, you've put me in a terrible situation."

"How so, my lord?"

The bishop looked as if he had been called upon to explain something self-evident. "Now that I know, I feel obligated to do something about it. Meanwhile, Brother Lorenzo and the others want me to treat her as if she were an immediate danger to the community, an agent of the evil one or something. So, if she were to appear in public without her shackles, they would accuse me of all kinds of leniency and bias!"

"God forbid!" Paire Miquel regretted his outburst almost as soon as he said it.

"Between you and me, I think the woman is harmless enough. My real intention is to give her some kind of public penance to satisfy the masses and then grant her absolution and let everything go back to the way it was. For the life of me, I can't figure out what all the hullabaloo is about!"

"How did we get into this in the first place?" asked the priest.

"As best as I can figure it, a bunch of people with torches in their hands showed up in front of Curé Antoine's rectory, demanding that he do something about this stranger, this woman, who had gotten some people's noses out of joint. They couldn't seem to agree on who or what they thought she was, but they were certain that whatever she may or may not have done fell under the jurisdiction of the Church. Curé Antoine, at a total loss as to what to do, organized a prayer service to ward off evil spirits and sent an urgent messenger to me. I had no choice but to place her under arrest and convene a bishop's court of inquiry."

Paire Miquel looked puzzled. "But surely, this sort of thing has happened before. What made you so reluctant to proceed with this case?"

"For one thing, the timing couldn't be worse." Bishop Raymond was grateful to have someone in whom he could confide. "The war was devastating for both civil and ecclesiastical authorities down here. Everyone, at one time or another, was under suspicion for heresy or for just being in the way of some ambitious northerner. Even now, in peacetime, we know we are being watched for the smallest indication that we are disloyal or unorthodox in our religious practices. Curé Antoine has long tolerated the sporadic use of other, non-Roman liturgical rites, such as Mme. Balterra's Hispanic Rite, because he was of such little consequence as to be beneath the notice of the new lords. I supported him with my silence, secure in the belief that he was right, but when this case erupted, everything changed."

"How would you normally have treated such disturbances?" The redhaired priest was trying to envision another outcome.

"Oh, ecclesiastical courts are notoriously lenient. Investigations usually conclude that the accusations amount to nothing. Even if someone is found guilty of something, the worst you could have expected of us was quick public penance. But most people have short memories. Most of the time, we drag things out until one of the parties dies or public interest is captured by something else. Then everything is forgotten, and we move on."

"But this case is different…" Paire Miquel could see how quickly something like this could spin out of control.

"Indeed, it is," replied Bishop Raymond. "The new count de Toulouse would not believe that I didn't know what was going on in a small parish under my jurisdiction. I had to distance myself from Curé Antoine, although I knew he had done nothing wrong. I had to give credence to all of these charges and to pretend that there was something there when there wasn't."

"But do you have the stomach to sacrifice a woman's freedom, and perhaps her life, to maintain the status quo?"

"I pray to God that I shall never find out! What do you want me to do about her shackles?"

"Have them removed," Paire Miquel replied. "At least in her cell, where nobody sees her but the gaolers and me, she can walk free. The gaolers can be bribed for their silence. When you bring her out to court, have the chains put back on, but gently."

Bishop Raimond agreed, and Paire Miquel went about his task with renewed determination.

CHAPTER 6

Mme. Senorant, Pascale's mother, had been taking care of Aidor since the unfortunate woman's arrest. Paire Miquel visited the home of Mme. Senorant to pick up Aidor and bring him to the Balterra farm. The boy seemed to be adjusting well, and he was delighted to able to spend time with his friend, but he was concerned about his mother. He didn't waste any time to so inform the priest and ask for any details about her condition that he could get out of him.

The priest was careful to edit his answers so as not to alarm the boy. "She's fine and eating as well as can be expected under the circumstances. She misses you terribly and is very anxious to know how you're getting on with Mme. Senorant."

"Tell her not to worry. Madame treats me kindly, and I love being able to be with Pascale every day. Only, I'd like to know when I can go home and feed the animals and be with Mother! I don't want to hear them say all those terrible things about her!"

"I will do my best to get her back for you as soon as I can," the priest said in a soothing tone, "but first you must help me. You must tell me about all of your mother's visitors, what they talked about and what they did."

"I'll do my best," said the boy. They were traveling on two horses, borrowed from M. Senorant, and they fell silent while appreciating the beauty of the countryside.

The foothills of the Pyrenees stretched out before them, a study in contrasts: hill and valley, shadow and light, trees and shrubs, cool breezes and stillness, much as it had been for as long as men have inhabited this region. The dwellings were all small, their roofs thatched and discolored by sun, wind, and rain. The fields rose and fell like wrinkled carpets strewn on either side of them. The people did not look up from their work, except for the occasional glance of passing curiosity.

Paire Miquel reminded himself that in this tiny corner of the wide world, everyone knew everyone else's business, including the trial in nearby Lescar, but still, the sight of a priest and a boy traveling by horseback must have stimulated a certain level of curiosity about the nature and mission of their journey.

As they climbed higher towards the distant mountains, every patch of rock seemed to be spouting a trickle of water, a fresh gurgling stream, inviting them to refresh themselves. They stopped to water their horses.

"It won't be long, now," speculated Paire Miquel, his line of sight blocked by the encroachment of hills.

"No, it won't," said the boy, standing up on his stirrups to get a better perspective. "See that hill over there where the sheep were just wandering, looking for tall grass? Well, just to the right, there's a sheep path that leads to where you can wade over the gave d'Oloron and descend into the valley. Then you turn right, proceed on that side of the river just a little bit, and you're there."

They were tired, and they indulged themselves with a long drink from the gurgling stream.

"They say the Blessed Mother loves this countryside," the boy remarked with a pensive expression, "...and that is why she has given us so many refreshing streams."

"We are truly blessed, that's for sure, though the soil's filled with embedded rock and very difficult to get through," commented the priest.

"With the monks, over at the Abbey de Sauvelade, is where you live, isn't it?"

"Temporarily," said the boy's absentminded adult companion. "You don't see many people out here, do you?"

"Other than shepherds, no, particularly when no one will talk to you, except for Pascale."

"What about the people who ask your mother for help?"

"I'm not usually allowed to be around when there are people, at our home, for consultation. Sometimes I'm outside in the garden, or when it's raining, I go into the chapel."

Paire Miquel perked up. "Tell me about what you see in the chapel."

"There's a big door at the front, but then no windows except for a huge round one on the back wall, and a whole bunch of candles and an altar covered by a white cloth, with a little box in front of it for kneeling. The altar has a cross on it, but not a regular one like you'll find at the village church. This one has four equal arms and fancy carving at the end of each arm. There are no paintings or anything, but the Book is on a stand to one side of the altar, all by itself."

"The Book," repeated the priest. "What does it look like?"

"It's big and thick, and I'm not allowed to pick it up. And it's got these funny, squiggly marks, that I can't read, all over it."

"Can your mother read it?" asked Paire Miquel.

"I think so," answered the boy, looking not so sure of himself. "But she said that Grandma and Grandpa could read it and that it was very holy to them back in Al Andaluse. Sometimes the friars who gave us Eucharist could read it, but they never told me what it was."

"To the best of your knowledge, did any of the people who came to your mother for help ever look at it?"

"No, no one, except once, when it was raining, I saw Curé Antoine come into the chapel with Mother and flip through the pages. He looked mostly confused, and he didn't look happy!"

"Here we are," said the priest. He dismounted and used the key Mme. Senorant had given him to release the lock on the wooden portail (gate). The place was windswept and overgrown with weeds. Dirt and blown leaves were everywhere. The front door stood ajar, and the dirt and leaves had accumulated in the doorway as if hoping for some shelter. The boy stood open-mouthed, as if, as St. Matthew had written, an enemy had sown weeds among the wheat. The place displayed more than human neglect; it showed the rampage of invaders bent on defiling the place.

Aidor ran to what had once been neat little beds in the garden. Now what herbs could still be found had been overpowered and choked by weeds gently swaying in the breeze. The priest strode over to join him and asked if he might be of assistance.

"There be days of work here to rid these beds of the weeds, and I don't rightly know if, in pulling out the weeds, we may uproot the good herbs themselves."

"Another day, perhaps," said the priest, for whom finding a cure for the injuries of Mme. Balterra was the higher priority. "I need for you to find me some dill and then meet me in the tool shed."

The boy looked puzzled at such a request, but he made for the nearby garden beds, murmuring, "Oc, mon paire."

Paire Miquel approached, entered the unlocked shed, and took stock of its contents. He found a crowded workbench on the window side of the wooden structure. On it was an array of beakers and bottles, some full and some empty, and a disused mortar and pestle such as a chemist might use to mix medicines. Presently Aidor entered with a handful of dill.

"Put it in the vessel over here." The priest was preoccupied, and he looked neither at the dill in the boy's outstretched hand nor at the receptacle for which it was intended. In fact, he was fascinated at having found so complete a chemical laboratory in so remote and desolate a place. Everywhere were tinctures and solutions of one thing or another. In an oak barrel in one corner, he thought he recognized the release valve used to regulate the pressure caused by the distillation of some vegetative substances into alcohol. Labels, of course, were conspicuous by their absence, and Paire Miquel could only conclude that this was attributable to the fact that except for Aidor, who acted as an assistant, only one chemist entered or worked here.

Aidor waited for what seemed like a long time while the priest took it all in. "What do you want me to do, Paire?" The boy's face wore a puzzled expression.

"Where does your mother keep her distilled alcohol?" asked the priest, in his turn.

"That would be this bottle over here," said the boy, eager to help. Aidor poured a little into the vessel containing the dill and proceeded to mash the contents until the dill was reduced to exceedingly small particles suspended in the alcohol. He then poured the tincture into a small bottle and handed it to the priest.

"Very good!" said the priest, slipping the bottle into a small sack tied around his waist. He deliberately didn't tell the boy what it was for, so as not to alarm him. He pointed to another small bottle on a shelf next to the boy and asked him to pass it over. The liquid in the bottle was a pale red, like watered-down wine. "I wonder what this is," he muttered to himself as he stowed the bottle in the small, leather sack he carried around his waist.

They strode outside, both quite pleased with themselves, when, on the spur of the moment, the priest turned to the little stone chapel and beckoned the boy to accompany him.

Paire Miquel pushed open the rain-swollen, heavy oak door and stood for a moment at the entrance, allowing time for his eyes to adjust to the gloom. After his first tentative steps, he could hear the shuffling gate of Aidor, who had entered behind him and breathed in the stale air of the place. The fragrance of burnt-out candles assaulted their senses, while everything else seemed dim and unreal. The round, central window was covered in dust, which meant that there was precious little light to illuminate the bare walls and the altar. However, it was not toward the altar that Paire Miquel turned. Rather, he spun toward a little lectern to its left, in pursuit of the open book that lay upon it.

Yes, that was it! This was the book that had come all the way from Hispania, written in the Latin Vulgate but transliterated in Arabic characters, the book that no one would touch but that everyone would talk about! The scholar-priest brushed his outstretched figures against the open pages as if he were paying homage to a treasure of incalculable value. He was able to make out a sentence once his eyes had adjusted to the darkness.

Omnes qui est ex veritate audit vocem   All who are of the truth hear my voice.
meam.

He knew what this meant, but would they believe it, coming from such a book?

Aidor just gazed, open-mouthed, up at the priest, who stood for what seemed like a long time, murmuring the arcane words, and looking very thoughtful. He didn't know whether the priest was pleased or angry. Then suddenly, as if he just made up his mind about something, the priest closed the book, picked it up, and stashed it under his arm. "Let's get out of here before we attract undue attention."

The two travelers left by horseback, as they had come, only, instead of returning directly to the Senorant home, where Pascale's mother would be waiting for them, they stopped at the Abbey de Sauvelade, where Paire Miquel handed the book to the abbot for safekeeping until he should call for it. He explained to the abbot that he required the services of two dependable monks to make the journey to Toledo and back, where they would make the acquaintance of a certain Hispanic scholar and return with him. They were to be careful not to disclose either their whereabouts or their mission to anyone. Upon their return, they were to report only to him. That being said, he and the boy left, feeling very relieved to have unburdened themselves of the treasure.

Aidor was puzzled. "What's all the fuss about the Book, anyway?"

"It's a valuable piece of evidence," replied the priest, "of which I'm surprised that Brother Lorenzo has not yet availed himself. It must be that the people who arrested your mother didn't venture into the chapel for some superstitious reason or another and that our prosecutor was so confident of the hearing's outcome that he was in no hurry to lay his hands on it. Maybe he had some reservations himself about handling the book. In any event, it's ours now, and all we need is someone whose word will be more readily taken than my own to silence our accusers by reading it."

"Do you mean that the book has a magic spell that will silence all its doubters?" The boy's eyes were wide with wonderment.

"No," said the priest, but knowledge of the book's contents will effectively silence your mother's accusers." They rode on without further conversation for a time while the boy digested all this.

CHAPTER 7

That evening, Paire Miquel returned to the cell of Teresa Balterra with his bottle of skin ointment, some fresh fruit and bread, and some news about the case. He was pleased to find his client unshackled and with a little bit of food, albeit unappetizing, set to the side. Unshackled, she was even able to wash superficially and to comb the brambles and clumps of dirt from her raven-dark hair. This did wonders for her state of mind and her willingness to dispute the charges against her.

The priest soothed her wounds with the proffered ointment. Her first reaction was a twinge of pain, but that was followed by a deep sigh of both physical and psychological relief. "It feels so good when it stops," she said with a weak smile.

"A counter-irritant," replied the priest, hoping that it helped more than it hurt.

"Not at all," she retorted, again smiling reassuringly. "After the stinging stops, it's like a second skin."

"What is this red tincture that I spotted this afternoon on a shelf next to your workbench?"

"Oh, that's just a little something I gave to Mme Barroux for her husband. He's something of a favorite with the ladies, or so I understand."

Paire Miquel changed the subject to a matter that had been very much on his mind. "What was the nature of your involvement with Malin, the blacksmith, and his daughter."

"Margo came to see me one evening after her father had evidently gone on some drunken rampage or another and then stumbled off to his forge to sober up and become suitably penitent. She had evidently been beaten repeatedly on the arms, the shoulders, the mouth, and the cheeks. I was horrified when I saw her. I immediately applied some soothing dill ointment to her injuries and encouraged her to talk to me about the whole situation."

"What did you learn?"

"Malin is a beast! He drinks until he loses control, and then he preys on those too frightened or awed by his authority to defend themselves."

"Was there a way that you could help her?" asked the priest, a look of complete disgust on his face.

"When Malin is sober, he is manageable, but when he drinks… I knew she had to get out of there. Another young lady had come to see me about a love potion to gain the attention of a nice young man of respectable circumstances in the village. Actually, there's really no such thing as a love potion. We give something to the lovers to give them enough confidence to do what they want to do anyway, and they credit the potion with their success. Anyway, I knew that the cabinetmaker's son was available, so I arranged for Margot and him to meet one evening under the pretext of separate consultations, and nature did the rest. It's a wonderful thing…nature. People underestimate its power all the time!"

"Of course, that did not endear you either to Malin or to the other young lady…whom I believe to have been a baker's assistant."

"You do your research well, mon paire," Teresa said with a slight smile of appreciation. "Loïsa is now engaged to the tinsmith's son and, to all appearances, is quite happy about it. As for Malin, I wouldn't waste a minute worrying over how he feels about anything."

"His name is on Fra Lorenzo's list of witnesses against you," commented the priest.

"No godly court would take that drunkard's word for anything resembling the truth!" declared the woman, displaying remarkable spirit for her condition of incarceration.

· · ·

The next day saw the resumption of the hearing and the calling of witnesses. Finally, Mme. Barroux would have her day in court to give her testimony. Paire Miquel had made an effort to interview her about her story, but she had been unwilling to receive him once she learned that he wished to speak with her in his capacity as Mme. Balterra's advocate.

Nevertheless, he was prepared to have this complicated story out in the open and to learn the extent of Mme Barroux's animosity toward his client.

Fra Lorenzo called his witness, and she processed to the dock with her heavy hips and dignity intact, without ever once glancing at the newly shackled woman and the red-haired priest at her side. Brother Lorenzo rose amid a ripple of freshly pressed robes and began his interrogation in halting Langue d'Oc, in keeping with Bishop Raymond's ruling.

"Mme Barroux, when did you first encounter Mme Balterra, here present?"

"It was about three years ago, my lord, when I went to her in all innocence, looking for advice and help."

"I am not your lord, Madame. I am your brother," Lorenzo said with a squinting, sour expression on his face. "What sort of advice or help did you require?"

"I wanted to have a baby. I know I'm getting on in years, but I still have my monthly bleeding, and I know it's possible. My son will one day set up a home of his own, and my husband was…less interested in me than when we were younger and less well established than we are now, the only reputable cabinetmakers in the Bearne region."

"So, you thought that having a baby would make your husband…more attentive, or at least, more available of evenings. Is that it?"

"Yes, my l…brother, he's a good man most of the time, and I know that he has a strong sense of duty."

"And how did this involve Mme. Balterra?" demanded Fra Lorenzo, bringing the focus back to the accused.

"I had heard that she mixed very effective concoctions and that she could help people successfully conceive and safely have a baby, so I went to ask her for help."

"What did she do for you?" asked Fra Lorenzo, anxious to get to Teresa's part in this drama.

"She prepared a mixture of myrtle leaves and water to soften my passages, but she also recommended a secret potion for my husband to…enliven his libido and increase his interest in intercourse. She said I was to have him drink it with his dinner and then encourage him to relax.

She said not to worry. That worry is the enemy of fertility, and that God would see to it that we would have our desire when we were ready."

"Did you do as Mme. Balterra told you to?" pressed Fra Lorenzo.

"Yes…and no," Mme. Barroux replied with some degree of embarrassment. "I was impatient to have it done, so I prepared my husband's treatment morning and evening, and I doubled my own dosage of myrtle and water."

"Did it work?"

"Yes,…but…"

"But?" Fra Lorenzo was clearly leading her to a new revelation.

Mme. Barroux began talking faster, with a frantic, hopeless note in her voice. "After the pregnancy, I saw less and less of my husband. He was not any too pleased about the prospect of a new baby, and he took to going out with the boys for a pastis or two after work. I would not see him sometimes until he returned well after dark, stinking drunk, sullen and moody. The next thing I knew, he was not coming home at all, but spending the night with a little putain he met at the tavern. Then he moved out and disappeared, with his strumpet, I presume!"

"And how did this involve Mme. Balterra?" pursued the prosecutor.

"'T'was she gave me the drops what would make him more amorous and attentive! She what had him under the influence of her potions while entering the world of trollops and barmaids! She knew he would do what he done! She ruined my family, she did!"

"Then?" asked Fra Lorenzo, looking for more evidence of Teresa's malevolence toward the Barroux family.

"She introduced my son to that silly child at the forge, and before I knew it, he married her, and I was left alone with a new baby and nobody to help, nobody! I hate that meddling witch, I do! I'll see her punished for what she done to my family, my happiness!"

Fra Lorenzo returned to his seat, a slight smile on his weasel-like face. "I have no further questions of this witness, my lord."

Paire Miquel rose slowly from the table, against which the chained Mme. Balterra leaned her heavy shackles. He smiled pleasantly at the witness and repeated back to her what she had already testified. "You have testified that you wished to have a baby?"

"Yes, mon paire. I hadn't known that joy since my son, my Bernard, was born, some twenty years ago."

The priest looked thoughtful. "Despite the danger to you and the child of a pregnancy at your age."

"Surely, I come from hardy stock, and I enjoy robust health, as you can see! Besides, Mme. Balterra assured me that she would take good care of me, be my midwife—and do the delivering herself, she would!"

"So, you considered it a risk worth taking?"

The priest was leading her somewhere, but she couldn't determine where he was going with this line of questioning. "Well, it was for my family! My son would surely be getting married one day, and my husband, you know, my husband was delivering furniture to every household what had a pretty daughter, and he would linger so, when I needed him to be with me, don't you see. He'd lost interest in me, and I had to get him back!"

"And you thought that having a child would bring him back to you?"

"He's not a bad man, Paire, quite charming when he wants to be. I knew he would consider it his duty to raise his child and, if it were a boy, to teach him a trade. He wouldn't walk away from that until *she* came along and fed him a love potion that just tore him from his hearth and home!"

"You mean, Mme. Balterra, to whom you had turned for help."

"I went to see her, even though others told me not to, and I begged her to help me have a baby and deliver it safely. I pleaded with her to help keep my family together, and this is what she has given me for my trouble."

"She did give you medicines and the services of a midwife," the priest restated from the previous testimony.

"Not at first. At first, she said it was dangerous and that keeping a husband at home was not a good reason for wanting a baby. Most of the time, she said, it doesn't work so well for the wife, and it just adds another reason for discontent and strife. All the time, she was planning to send him away to his little whore and leave me with nothing."

"You have your baby," said the priest, stating what he thought was obvious.

"My baby was born a cripple, with one leg shorter than the other and turned in, like a beggar. I ended up with a crippled girl whom nobody would want as a wife, a burden for me to raise and support all the days of my life."

"And you think that the myrtle water and the medicine Mme. Balterra gave you for your husband caused that?"

"They were cursed," said the grief-stricken mother, "and you can't prove that they weren't."

The priest thought for a moment. "I don't imagine that even my learned colleague over there could prove that my horse did not speak to me on the way from the abbey to court this morning, but I hardly think that his lordship would accept Fra Lorenzo's failure to do so as evidence that the horse had, indeed, spoken!"

There followed general laughter in the courtroom, but Mme. Barroux did not appear to follow. Paire Miquel decided to take his witness in another direction. "You believe that Mme. Balterra drove your husband into the arms of another woman with his medication?"

Mme. Barroux looked indignant at the priest's question. "Of course, she did. He took the medicine, and he went away with his hussy!"

"And yet you testified that he had committed marital infidelities *before* you decided to have a baby and seek help from Mme. Balterra."

"Oc, yes, but he never ran out before like that!"

Paire Miquel raised a different question. "How long had it been since you had had a new baby in the house?"

"My son, my Bernard, is twenty years old," Mme Barroux said with evident pride in her voice.

"A male child, not a disfigured child, one to whom he could teach a trade?"

"Yes," she said, looking thoughtful, perhaps regretful.

"And did he willingly take the potion to enhance his interest and give you more chances to conceive?"

"No, Paire. I concealed it in his morning and evening cup. He was unaware that I had ever provided it."

"So, he had no idea he had been given the potion?"

"No, mon paire. I didn't discuss it with him at all."

"And it was you, and not Mme. Balterra, who administered the potion?"

"Oc, mon paire," admitted the woman, although she did not appear to be following his line of thought.

"Had your husband, in fact, ever met Mme. Balterra?"

"Not to my knowledge. She does not frequent the kinds of taverns that my husband patronizes."

"Then she didn't have much opportunity to exert influence over him, did she?"

"Well, he did take the potion, didn't he?" demanded the woman with a great show of indignation.

"Is this, in fact, the potion that you gave him morning and evening?" Paire Miquel pulled a small bottle from around his waist and showed it to Mme. Barroux, Fra Lorenzo, and the bishop.

"Where did you get that?" Brother Lorenzo challenged upon seeing the look of surprise on Mme. Barroux's face.

"From Mme. Balterra's workbench, which my client asked me to visit in search of needed medicinal supplies. She later identified its contents as left over from the potion she had prepared for Mme. Barroux's husband. Do you recognize it, Madame?"

Mme. Barroux opened the bottle and lifted it to her nose. "Smells exactly like what I put in his drinks."

The priest retrieved the bottle, turned to the prosecutor, and lifted it so that everyone could see it. "I have a small laboratory back at the abbey, where I was able to examine the contents. Do you know what I found, Madame?"

"No, Paire," said the confused woman.

"It contains rose water, common rose water. Do you know the medicinal uses of rosewater, Madame?"

"You put it on your hands to soften the skin and to prevent or reduce inflammation."

"Precisely, and is it ever recommended or used as an aphrodisiac?"

"A what?" She was evidently unfamiliar with the word.

"As a love potion, Madame," prompted the priest.

"No, Paire," admitted the woman.

"My lord, the court may order its own experts to check this point, but as something of a specialist in alchemy, I can attest that rose water is nothing of the sort."

One of the other judges piped up long enough to give his officious comment: "As a student of alchemy myself, I stipulate, my lord, that rose water is not an aphrodisiac."

"Then, Mme. Barroux, I suggest that we have no evidence indicating that Mme. Balterra ever induced your husband to stray or, in fact, took any action that indicated animosity toward you or your family. Do you not agree, Madame?"

Mme. Barroux summoned all her dignity and maintained a stoic expression, but she said nothing.

"I have no further questions of this witness, my lord," said Paire Miquel before resuming his seat.

CHAPTER 8

The next day was market day in Bastanès, and as it was Thursday evening, most of the witness begged to be excused from court in Lescar on Friday, to be able to do their shopping back home. So, Bishop Raymond adjourned until the following Monday.

With Mme. Teresa Belterra confined to her cell, Paire Miquel borrowed a horse from the abbey and rode the short distance from Lescar to Bastanès in the hopes of learning more about his client as well as the prevailing mood of the local inhabitants.

The town center of Bastanès was dominated by a large pine and thatch-covered roof supported on four sides by enormous wooden pillars cut and transported from trees of considerable age and girth. Additional support pillars were strategically located near the center of the old structure and at intervals of thirty paces or so. The overall effect was that of a very large, open-walled barn, affording some shelter in the event of inclement weather. That day, however, what was usually open space was almost entirely taken up with tables, stalls, and displays, which made it impossible to walk in a straight line from one side to the other.

Everywhere were leather purses, saddlebags, boots, cinctures, cloaks, blouses, and jerkins of linen and wool. Paire Miquel followed his nose in the direction of fresh cuts of mutton, rabbit, and veal. The blood that dripped from the carcasses, which were suspended on hooks, taunted the dogs below. Tables displayed the produce of the harvest: leeks; lettuce; rich, ripe strawberries; cabbages; carrots; potatoes; and leaf spinach.

Despite the apparent chaos of products and vendors, the market was, in fact, carefully divided into sections reserved for the different trade guilds. To the north (which made Paire Miquel grateful for the west-to-east direction of the prevailing winds), at the far end of the pavilion, the fishmongers were installed, their Atlantic catch having traveled overland from Bayonne. To the east assembled the tinsmiths, with their pots, frying pans, saucepans, and colanders. Further west, the tanners raised a fragrance of their own with the fresh hides being dried and shaped for the making of all sorts of leather goods, which they did before your eyes. Behind them, the cloth merchants displayed their wares, more colorful and stylish than most of the peasants of Bastanès could afford to contemplate. The fruits and vegetables were tantalizingly displayed on the tables to the south with other delights, such as spices and perfumes, from Hispania and the outer Mediterranean countries. Women in exotic silk scarves and flowing gowns offered their products with coquettish smiles that induced even Paire Miquel to imagine other pleasures.

Paire Miquel appreciated the market, above all, as a human circus, where no one worried about tomorrow and where everything could and did happen at the least expected moment. The priest glanced at the stalls of the cloth merchants and spied a young girl sweeping a new scarf around her long neck and flashing her pleasure for the eyes of a young man, who had, no doubt, just disposed of a month's wages to give it to her. Showing never a moment's remorse, he could not have been more pleased with himself to see her so happy with the gift. In another corner, three children hid themselves, waiting for the purveyor of sweets to turn to the aid of a prospective customer before they crept up to the counter and raced away with a stolen handful of treasure. Paire Miquel did not pursue the culprits but sauntered up to the table of sweets and intentionally overpaid for two bonbons of honey and caramel.

Off to one side, another young couple took advantage of their new-found refuge from the bustle of the crowds to steal an embrace and the unspoken promise of groping hands and quickened breath. It was not, however, the young couple that arrested Paire Miquel's attention at that instant, but the spectacle of a ponderous horse-drawn wagon that stood by itself, off to one side and away from the cover of the pavilion, at the entrance to a lonely side street.

The wagon was ill-kept and shabby, much like its driver, who sat aloft in a ragged pair of mid-calf length, canvas trousers, a stained green and white shirt, and a red bandana around his neck. On his head, he wore a woolen cap whose pointed crown drooped to one side, with no other purpose than to cover his balding head. His cart displayed a crude, handmade sign with a simple red and white pole, identifying him as a barber.

As Paire Miquel looked on, one man came up to the barber and entered the wagon's enclosed cabin through the back. The barber had been sharpening his razor as the man came up, and he took it with him as he joined him inside.

As the priest had nothing better to do, he waited, and ten minutes later, the visitor emerged, still sporting an untrimmed beard but with a piece of white cloth wrapped around his left arm, which he seemed to be favoring. The priest concluded that the barber had subjected the man to a bleeding—no doubt, to restore the balance of his bodily humors. Hence the red stripes on his pole. For his part, the visitor re-entered the market to reward himself with a bottle of wine to replenish his body fluids.

There weren't very many other visitors to the barber's wagon that morning, either for shaves, haircuts, or miscellaneous medical treatments. As merchants busied themselves with replenishing their stands and rearranging their products, the barber just sat there, sharpening his razor and looking forlorn. Paire Miquel was about to approach the barber to introduce himself, when he saw a cheerful, plump man in a black cassock and round-brimmed hat gleefully sauntering in his direction from one of the fresh fruit stands. He was looking very pleased with himself. Although the two men did not know one another, they recognized the distinct attire of clergymen, and that gave them something in common.

Paire Miquel learned that his companion was none other than Curé Antoine of the tiny local parish of St. Martin. The smiling parish priest had made his way straight from morning Mass to the market, anxious to stock up on his one physical weakness: sweet fruits, the more exotic, the better. He could and would recite the litany of all the tropical fruits from Palestine, Syria, and Africa that made their way here by way of Islamic Hispania and could be hunted down like little treasures in the local markets. The vegetables, too, were good for winter storage since they were easier to preserve and, therefore, more plentiful than meats. Carrots and parsnips were good for thickening savory soups on cold winter evenings. He held two sacks, bulging with fresh produce.

Although Curé Antoine was very proud of his culinary discoveries and content to show them all to his new friend, along with detailed instructions on how to prepare each of them, Paire Miquel was not interested in discussing fruit or vegetables. With some impatience, he turned the subject to the bishop's notorious prisoner, Mme. Balterra. Curé Antoine had himself been to see Mme. Balterra on several occasions. Surely, he had availed himself of her teas and soothing solutions. Given his natural curiosity about the preparation of food and drink, hopefully, he could enlighten Paire Miquel as to their contents and usage,

"Yes, yes, yes, of course I visited her, several times. I wished to prepare young Aidor for the reception of the sacraments and to ensure that he learns the truths of the faith, as is my duty. Besides, my knees are not getting any younger, and they cause me terrible agony, especially when it's going to rain. She gave me an ointment to reduce the swelling, and it worked so well that I confess I came back for more...and to continue Aidor's lessons, of course.

"Of course," agreed Paire Miquel, "and what was in that ointment?"

"A mixture of eucalyptus and Spanish olive oil, I am told," replied the parish priest, "and it worked like magic!"

"You didn't use that word to describe it to anyone else, did you?"

"Well, I guess I did, but I meant it as hyperbole, you realize."

"Yes, *I* realize how you meant it," replied the priest-scholar, a dubious frown on his face. "Did Mme. Balterra give you anything else?"

"Why, yes. She prepared an herbal tea for me. She said it would help me sleep, regardless of the pain." Curé Antoine seemed almost apologetic for having accepted the tea.

"Did she tell you which herbs she used?" Pair Miquel saw a look of surprise on the other priest's face, as if he would never have thought to ask such a thing.

"Certainly not! Healers are permitted their professional secrets. Such a question would have been considered impertinent."

"And yet much of the case against her now has to do with the nature of her concoctions."

"I saw no harm in it," confessed the curé, "I still see no harm in it."

"And yet you haven't said so in open court." Paire Miquel's voice was somewhat accusatory.

"The opinion of a poor, unschooled parish priest does not carry much weight around here compared to that of a renowned scholar such as yourself." Curé Antoine wore a hurt and defensive look.

It had occurred to Paire Miquel to call the parish priest as a character witness, and he was anxious to learn more and give him an opportunity to speak his mind, but Curé Antoine spied a table, visible over Miquel's shoulder, where a woman was fussing over a new display of ripe figs from one of the local orchards. The parish priest of Bastanès had a particular passion for "figues," and he saw that Mme. Malin, the blacksmith's wife, was hovering about the stand, no doubt waiting for her husband, who usually made a beeline for the figs and bought them all before anyone else had a chance.

After waiting with some impatience, Mme. Malin left the stand, in search of her husband. Abruptly Curé Antoine excused himself from further time-consuming conversation and made haste for the fig stand.

CHAPTER 9

Paire Miquel's conversation with the parish priest thus concluded, he decided to resume his visit to the barber's coach. The barber's wagon looked like a grossly oversized, cylindrical wine keg, secured on top of a flat bed. Two tired horses were hitched close to the front two of the wagon's four enormous wheels. As there was, at that moment, no one in the vicinity, Paire Miquel hopped onto the back step of the vehicle with the aid of a small stool that had been left there for that purpose, and he knocked on the rear door.

"Go away!" came a voice from the inside, above what must have been panting and moaning in both male and female vocal registers. Paire Miquel, realizing the delicacy of the moment and backed away from the door and onto the ground. No sooner had he touched the ground, when Claude Fouquet, the barber, unwilling, on further reflection, to lose one of the few customers he still had, came to the door, still pulling up his trousers. The two men looked at each other, both not even trying to disguise their disdain and disappointment. Paire Miquel was clearly not a customer, and Fouquet was making no effort to hide his annoyance. Miquel closely examined the barber's face and concluded that he was a practical man. Now that his passionate tryst had been spoiled, the barber/surgeon might be looking for what advantage there might be from this encounter.

Fouquet's reaction was not what Paire Miquel expected, but neither was the identity of the female figure who emerged from his door, a little disheveled but otherwise self-composed. Miquel immediately recognized her as Adelle Malin, the blacksmith's wife. Her narrow brown eyes had a wariness about them and a look of defiance that he frequently encountered in those who knew they had done something wrong but refused to repent. She looked as if she had a story to tell. With great misgivings, the priest entered the barber's compartment.

Paire Miquel took a moment to adjust his sight to the vaulted chamber's pervasive state of obscurity. The first object to catch his eye was a long table on which the client would recline for a haircut, shave, or bleeding. Next to the long table was a chair, and beside the chair was a smaller stand containing an array of instruments. Discretely hidden under the table was a bucket to catch the flow of blood. Candles, sparingly placed here and there, lent a gloomy half-light to the place. Another table, against the opposite wall, displayed an array of bottles: herbs, tonics, solutions, and tinctures, the mainstay of the barber's curative trade, all carefully labeled.

"These tonics and tinctures cure everything from toe itch to syphilis sores," proclaimed Fouquet, his head held high, his hand sweeping across his varied inventory. Paire Miquel saw that the products were grouped by function: St. Paul's potion for epilepsy and stomach problems; ox gall and urine for leg pain; snail slime for burns; bull's gall, onion, and garlic for eye infections; roasted owl and boar's grease for gout; catgut, hedgehog grease, and bear fat for sore throat; and an empty bottle of belladonna to make women's eyes more alluring to men.

"I just sold the last of that to one of my few remaining female customers," admitted Fouquet. "Business is not good these days, with that gypsy-witch selling her foreign remedies just on the other side of town."

"Nor do your remedies look altogether wholesome and safe," added the priest, looking skeptically at what was lined up before him. "So, you have no sympathy for Mme. Balterra's plight at all, do you?"

"Not in the least! A man has to make a living, doesn't he? I don't suppose you'd welcome another church set up on the other side of the village, would you now?"

"I live in a monastery that supports my studies and experiments. I don't get much involved in parish affairs myself, and I move around a great deal." The priest's answer was more informational than argumentative.

"Anyway," said the barber, "if she wants to live by herself and grow food to feed her and her son, God bless her, but when she starts giving medicines to my customers, I take exception. You know what I mean!"

Paire Miquel was about to answer when a noise arose from the market outside, the sound of a man speaking in a loud and frightened voice. Others responded with high-pitched screams. Both Fouquet and Paire Miquel rushed to the door and leapt down to the ground to see what was happening.

Chaos was the only word that adequately described the scene that met their eyes in the marketplace. Overturned tables and stands spewed their various produces over the ground. Open cages released live chickens and geese, who were running and squawking in fright from the scene. Alarmed onlookers backed away as a wild-eyed man in a black cassock rolled on the ground, clutching his throat, trashing nearby table legs with his feet and incoherently screaming, as far as either Fouquet or Paire Miquel could see, at no one in particular. The victim's clerical collar had been loosened from around his neck, but both men recognized Curé Antoine. Paire Miquel listened carefully in an effort to understand the significance of what Antoine's panicked voice was trying to say.

"Get away from me! Get away! Don't let them touch me. Snakes, snakes! Get them away from me! I feel them creeping all over me. Stop! Make them stop! Please, please!" With much difficulty, he rose to his feet and staggered towards the nearest exit from the square. His eyes were bulging, and his face was twisted in terror and disgust. His breathing was shallow and labored, and his trembling hand found the leather band of the pectoral cross around his neck. With what seemed unnatural force, he yanked the cross from about his neck and threw it to the ground. The frightened onlookers moaned in unison and moved back as if all under the same command.

Through eyes seared by the sun and yielding only vague and moving images, Antoine spied for the first time the wavering figure of Paire Miquel. "Michaelus, Michaelus, stop them, stop them, please!" But before the scholar-priest could reach his new friend, the hapless victim collapsed to the ground, seized by bone-rattling convulsions, and then he lay still.

Paire Miquel ran to him, stooped, and felt for a pulse, but he could find no sign of life. A stream of thick blood and saliva dripped from the corner of the curé's mouth, and his eyes were gaping, the pupils fixed and fully dilated. Paire Miquel carefully pushed closed his friend's eyelids and raised his own hand in the sign of the cross. Intoning the Latin formula for absolution, he consigned the curé's soul to his Creator. A momentary silence fell over the crowd.

Suddenly Adelle Malin, who was also standing near them, let out an ear-rattling screech and pointed to the limp body on the ground. "He was bewitched! The evil one has taken possession of our priest. Only the witch could have conjured him to do this. Did he not act like a madman, like one possessed, someone who had totally lost control of his senses? She is laughing at us from her prison cell, that evil doer, that busybody! She must be punished for this MURDER!"

Paire Miquel could see that the crowd was being worked into a frenzy and that he was in no position to predict what the outcome might be. With the help Malin's young apprentice, he hoisted up the limp body of Curé Antoine and carried him into the church.

The boy Esteve was anxious to find out what was happening out on the street and immediately returned to see what he could find out. Paire Miquel used the relative silence of the church to examine the body.

The red-haired priest furrowed his brow and looked at the ashen face as if waiting for answers. How could the fit have come about so suddenly? One minute, a jovial, peaceful man is shopping for fruits and vegetables, and the next, a raving lunatic screams incoherently, throws himself on the ground, and dies! It defies logical explanation. Was it the onset of madness, demonic possession, the agency of evil intervention? Clearly, this could not have occurred without some sort of external agency!

"External agency!" The priest jerked his head and placed his hand on the dead man's chin. "What is this blistering and rash on the man's lips?" He racked his brain, trying to remember what might cause such a thing. "Something he drank or ate?" Hastily, he removed the dead priest's cassock to look for other signs of a rash. As he gently lifted the arms, he noted the same redness and blistering on the tips of the fingers on the corpse's right hand.

"So," concluded the priest-scholar, "Curé Antoine took something in his hand and raised it to his mouth, and thus, he self-administered the...POISON!" He rushed out of the church and headed not into the still unruly market, but to the barber's wagon. He pushed open the back door without knocking and found Fouquet rummaging through his bottles and beakers, a bottle of tranquilizing tonic on a three-legged stool beside him. The priest made straight for the table of medicines and quickly identified the empty bottle of Belladonna. Bottle in hand, he swung over to the long table and shook the barber in an effort to gain his undivided attention. "To whom did you sell this and when?" The priest's eyes were steady and unmoving. His lips were sealed shut in an earnest grimace.

"How dare you barge into my wagon as if you own the place! First, you interrupt my lovemaking. Then you disturb my work. For what? To ask me the name of one of my few remaining clients? That's nerve, I'll tell you!"

"This is called belladonna, isn't it? Do you know by what other name it is called?"

"No, and I don't care," answered the still annoyed and determinedly uncooperative barber.

"It's called deadly nightshade, and it's a particularly useful poison."

"What's that got to do with me? I didn't poison anybody!"

"I believe it has something to do with the death of Curé Antoine," said the priest, now in a calmer tone of voice, trying to win over the barber's cooperation.

"Everybody says that he was bewitched by that Saracen bitch that the bishop has currently locked up in Lescar. She'll get what's coming to her now, I'll wager!"

"I have reason to believe that she didn't do it. Curé Antoine was poisoned with belladonna," said the priest, more certain than ever that his hypothesis was correct. "Belladonna leaves a red rash, if left in contact with the skin."

"Why would one of my customers want to poison a priest?" asked Fouquet.

"I don't know," said Paire Miquel, "but that's something I'd like to find out."

"Well, he looked to me like a man bewitched, and I have no intention of helping you get that witch off."

"If you don't help me," the priest pleaded, "an innocent woman may be put to death for a crime she did not commit!"

"And why should I care for which crimes she is punished? She's a witch, isn't she?"

"The fact that you want Mme. Balterra blamed, coupled with your resentment of her as a rival, gives you a motive to kill Curé Antoine and encourage the chorus of her accusers."

"Get out! Get out of here! You're not the appointed keeper of the peace. I don't have to violate the confidentiality of my few remaining customers for a man who stands there and accuses me of murdering a priest!"

"We shall see," said Paire Miquel. "I shall pray for your soul," he added on his way out the door.

CHAPTER 10

Back in the marketplace, Paire Miquel saw that the crowd, now somewhat muted as the shock set in, had gathered into different groups to discuss the matter. As soon as Esteve, the apprentice, spied Paire Miquel, he came up to the red-haired priest with two sacks of groceries in his hands.

"I found these in the street. Curé Antoine must have dropped them when the madness seized him."

Paire Miquel took them to a nearby bench in a shady spot to one side of the market. "Thank you," he said. "Let's see what we've got here. Yes, these are the treasured vegetables and exotic fruits that he showed me. But where are the figs? He left me to go buy some figs. Where are they?"

"Maybe he ate them," postulated Esteve, thinking himself quite clever.

"Not all of them," speculated the priest, "even if he was something of a *gourmand*. I'll bet someone picked them up. I'd like to get my hands on them."

"It's a shame to waste good figs, said the boy, his grin of satisfaction not shared by the priest.

Paire Miquel slumped on the bench, at a loss as to what to do next. "What else have you learned?" he asked, his voice weary and concerned.

"One of the village men took to horse to inform the authorities in Toulouse about the murder. I'm afraid the count's military detachment will be here by Monday to take over the investigation."

"That's not good news!" Paire Miquel furrowed his brow. "We haven't had knights here since the Cathar Wars. They look for rebellion and disloyalty under every rock!"

"Someone reported that the bishop had taken off the witch's chains while she was confined to her cell, and a delegation has gone back to

Lescar to demand that the court order her re-shackled," commented Esteve, not considering how the news might be taken by her counsel.

At that moment, Paire Miquel spotted a familiar figure lurking around the disserted stands in hopes of finding a stray piece of honey candy.

"Pascale Senorant!" called out the priest, having caught the boy in the act of pilfering. Aidor Balterra's only friend deftly concealed his hands behind his back.

The boy walked slowly over to the priest while stealthily secreting a piece of candy into his shirt. "I'm sorry, Paire. I thought nobody would miss it."

"I'm just concerned that you don't accidentally eat something that might not be good for you."

"I won't take any more, I promise!"

"Don't worry about that just now. Where's Aidor? I don't think he's particularly safe in this crowd."

"Aidor stayed home with my father. We thought that would be better. Mamon is right over there. I'll get her if you want."

The priest raised his hand. "That won't be necessary. I'll ask her about Aidor later. Were you and your mother at the market just now, when Curé Antoine…died?"

"Yes. Mamon was over at the boucher (butcher) examining the mutton, and I was with Esteve at the candy table." Please don't tell Mamon that I took some candy!"

"Never mind that. Do you remember seeing anything unusual or out of place?"

"Everybody was milling around, pushing, pointing, sampling, but that's not out of place for these kinds of markets."

"Do you remember seeing Curé Antoine?" pressed the priest, not quite sure what the boy should have noticed.

"No…yes, I saw him shift two sacks into one hand and use the other hand to stick something into his mouth."

"Did you happen to notice what he was eating?"

"Yes. They were figs. Big, black, juicy figs, and he smiled as if he had gone to Heaven and seen God."

"Did you see anything else?"

"I saw M. Malin, the blacksmith, looking at the priest and then toward the fruit stand where he had gotten the figs. There were none left."

"Did Malin approach Antoine?

"No, Curé Antoine just went crazy as if he were seeing things that the rest of us couldn't see. People started pushing in all directions to get away from him, and then he fell down and died!"

"What happened to the rest of the figs that Curé Antoine purchased?"

"I don't know. They must be in one of his grocery sacks."

The priest thought for a minute. "Esteve recovered those grocery sacks. Please find him and tell him to bring them to me. I'll meet him in the church. Go quickly."

Five minutes later, Paire Miquel and the apprentice were emptying the sacks onto one of the church's gloomy back pews. They found carrots, onions, cabbage, almonds, grapes, but no figs. Strange, thought Paire Miquel. "Did you find any figs on the ground," he asked, a puzzled look on his face.

"No, Paire," said the apprentice. He looked defensive, as if he were being accused of a lie.

"Did you or Pascale eat any of them?" The priest looked genuinely concerned rather than accusatory.

"Oh, no, Paire. Neither of us had ANYTHING except the candy, I swear!" protested the frightened boy.

"Don't swear!" said the priest, a little sharper than he intended. He quickly changed the subject. "We have to find out what became of those figs!"

"There'll be plenty more at next week's market, I'm sure," reflected the boy. Then he had a thought. "If I were you, I'd check with old man Malin about what happened to those figs, I would."

"You're not suggesting he would kill a priest over a bunch of figs, are you?"

"You don't know what a mean son of a...well, cruel fellow Malin is."

"I believe I do," said the priest, looking amused at Esteve's little slip.

Paire Miquel made a mental note to pay the blacksmith a visit, but first, he thought, he must get back to Lescar to check into Mme. Balterra's situation in the wake of these recent developments.

CHAPTER 11

Never before. in Paire Miquel's memory, had the town of Lescar more resembled a city under siege! Men had abandoned their fields, and the women their vegetable gardens, to stand before the bishop's residence en masse, pitchforks in hand, demanding that the witch be given the death penalty for her crimes. Angry voices could be heard even in the church, during public mass. The bishop said mass privately in his chapel lest he be accosted by hysterical onlookers during the sacred mysteries. Rumors had spread like locusts all through the town that the witch was unshackled and free to wave her arms and whisper incantations from her cell. The crowd demanded that she be restrained, and the bishop, in a panic, complied. He dreaded the resumption of proceedings on Monday since he could foresee no way to conduct an inquiry away from the influence of the unruly mob.

Men, women, and children were straining as if drawn by some external force, pushing and shoving each other inching closer and closer, as the scholar-priest mingled with the assembled masses edging toward the center of town and the bishop's residence. He recognized many of the farmers and burghers of Bastanès, the scene of the fateful market. They had made the journey, no doubt, in response to the horrendous spectacle of Curé Antoine's madness and death, which had taken place before their eyes. In fact, they spoke of little else, convinced as they were that they had witnessed nothing less than an unspeakable, demonic spell, called down on the hapless priest by the evil and resourceful witch whom the bishop held in custody.

"Did you know that the bishop ordered her unshackled?" an indignant woman asked rhetorically to anyone nearby who might not already know. "My cousin is one of the gaolers here, and he told me the old man actually took pity on her and left her at liberty in her cell to wave her arms about and send spells to the outer air. It's negligence, I'll tell you, and downright cowardice!"

Another neighbor smiled in agreement. "Maybe she'll kill him next. God knows only the devil would want to kill a godly man like our curé."

"What more evidence do we need to know that there is EVIL in our midst?" The question was raised by a young man, pitchfork in hand, with a fanatical expression on his face that announced to the world his rock-hard certainty.

The makeshift gaol was actually a converted shed on ecclesiastical property, to the rear of the bishop's residence. It was only people's reluctance to violate sanctuary that kept them at a distance. The handful of terrified-looking guards that the bishop had selected were in no way equal to the task of keeping the mob at bay should they choose to enter there. With difficulty, Paire Miquel separated himself from the crowd and made his way around back to the gaol.

"Teresa!" The red-haired priest couldn't restrain a cry of shock and horror as he saw the disheveled woman. She was chained to the wall in a sitting position, arms and legs immobilized, wrists and ankles in heavy iron clamps fastened to the wall by heavy chains. A dirty rag had been shoved into her mouth and securely tied behind her head. Restrained as she was, she was unable to stand, lie down, or cry out for help. Her rags were filthy with her own urine and feces, and her food dish, beside the lower sliding door at the entrance and thus out of reach, was lumpy, rancid, and covered with feasting flies and rodents. Her hair was unkept, and her face covered with flies, which she could not raise a hand to chase away.

The priest knelt beside her, unfastened her gag, and, with no shame, removed and replaced her clothing. Then he coaxed water and bread down her parched throat. She said that the gaolers had fallen upon her and accused her of the charmed murder of a priest. She was frightened for Paire Miquel and for herself, not knowing which priest was dead. The gaolers had restrained her as tightly as they could and told her there would be no further spells or incantations emanating from this place. Thus, had she stayed until Paire Miquel had arrived.

The red-haired priest told her about the murder of Curé Antoine and of the chaotic scene that had followed. He asked her whether she was in possession of any belladonna. She answered that she did not collect or stock it, since it was far too dangerous to have it in her shop, with Aidor having such easy access. Paire Miquel was relieved, and he confided his suspicions about the figs.

"Malin, the blacksmith, has a weakness for figs, you know," she added. "Every market day, Mme Malin buys him all that she can get hold of in order to put him in a better mood. Saves her from a beating or two, I suppose."

"That's very interesting," said the priest, making another mental note to pay the blacksmith a visit.

After encouraging a little more food and water down Mme. Balterra's throat, Paire Miquel excused himself, made his way as stealthily as possible to the rear of the bishop's residence and asked admittance from a servant. Having had the good fortune to have found a way to enter and leave unobserved, the scholar-priest decided to try his luck by asking to see the bishop. To his great surprise, he was ushered right in.

Paire Miquel found himself in the middle of an audience granted to Fra Lorenzo, wherein the monk was bringing his master up to date concerning the details surrounding Curé Antoine's demise. The bishop wore a worried countenance, but nothing like the panic and fanatical fever one could discern from the face of Brother Lorenzo.

"The man displayed all the classic symptoms of demonic possession: uncontrolled, spasmatic movement, panic, hallucination, and, I must add with some disgust in the telling, a sudden and urgent desire to be rid of his pectoral cross, a symbol of Christ Himself! Who but the devil could have driven him, a good man, a godly man, to commit such an act of sacrilege!"

"Has Fra Lorenzo examined Curé Antoine's body *post-mortem*?" asked the red-haired priest, having retained his composure despite the horrifying details of the case.

"Well, no," admitted the monk. "And I hope that my learned colleague is prepared to tell us that he has treated the body of a brother priest with the proper dignity!"

"Indeed, I have," returned the scholar-priest, "and I have found evidence of MURDER committed by a human agent, by a POISON known as belladonna."

"Despite all of the evidence you have just heard concerning demonic possession?"

"I can assure you that the documented symptoms of deadly nightshade poisoning can adequately explain all of Curé Antoine's bizarre behavior, including the difficulty with breathing that prompted him to tear off the pectoral cross."

"Who but the devil would target a representative of Christ and risk damnation of his soul by taking his life in such a gruesome way?"

"I don't know," admitted Paire Miquel, realizing that there were holes in his alternate method theory.

"Is there anyone but the devil who stood to gain from the death of the priest?"

"None that I can think of."

"And have you located a poisoned cup or tainted article of food?"

"Not as yet, although I have my suspicions," said the scholar-priest, unwilling to reveal all that he knew while the murderer could still destroy the evidence.

"Then I suggest that until we know WHO might have poisoned Curé Antoine, WHY he would do such a thing, WHAT he might hope to gain from doing so, and HOW he could possibly have administered the poison, we continue to adhere to the simple assumption that the good curé was bewitched!"

The bishop had become increasingly concerned about where this conversation was going. "Might I remind you both that the crime of MURDER is not under the jurisdiction of ecclesiastical courts but necessitates us to turn it over to the civil authorities in Toulouse!"

"My lord, this question has achieved even more urgency now that someone has sent for a garrison from Toulouse," said Paire Miquel, turning away for the moment from his alternate theory of the crime.

"I, for one, look forward to the arrival of a cadre of knights to help us control this unruly mob outside!" said the bishop, still trying to wish the whole thing away.

"Be careful what you wish for, my lord, for soldiers who are welcomed upon their arrival are seldom thanked when they leave, having helped themselves to our homes, our provisions, our wives and daughters, and a large part of our wine!"

"But knights nowadays live by a code of chivalry, do they not?" protested the bishop.

"A soldier is a soldier, and occupation is occupation, no matter how many pretty stories and ballads of brave and generous deeds come out of the court of Bordeaux and its imitators," Paire Miquel said with a note of bitterness in his voice. "We must prepare ourselves once again to undergo a military occupation and find ourselves treated as hostiles in our own town!"

"I think you overdramatize, Pater Michaelus," Lorenzo simpered. "We are all on the side of justice, are we not?"

"Yes, but who decides what justice is?" replied the scholar-priest. "Which brings me to my next subject. Is it 'just' to have the woman gagged and shackled until she is utterly helpless and unable to either manage her food or get up to take care of her own bodily functions? Does the Church practice 'justice' when it presupposes her guilt and commences her punishment BEFORE the completion of her trial? Surely, without food and proper care, she will DIE before your lordship has properly adjudicated this case!"

"But she MUST be restrained, lest her incantations occasion another MURDER," replied Fra Lorenzo. "Surely, you can see the logic of that decision!"

"It was never my intention to cause death or harm to the woman in any way!" protested the bishop, whom Lorenzo had kept uninformed about the true condition of his prisoner. "The purpose of an ecclesiastical court is to instruct, enlighten, and absolve, not to punish."

"I doubt that you will find the knights from Toulouse to be bearers of similar scruples, my lord," added the red-haired priest. "I suggest that we find a middle way between cruelty and freedom of movement before the soldiers take that decision from us."

The bishop turned to face Lorenzo. "See to it!" he ordered and dismissed the prosecutor with a wave of his hand.

Left alone with Paire Miquel, Bishop Raymond let out a deep sigh. "This matter will get out of hand before it's over, I'm afraid! With the mob baying for blood and men like Lorenzo all too willing to fan the flames, we may end up doing something that we will look back upon with shame and horror!"

"I beg you, my lord, keep this an ecclesiastical case, or there's no telling what violence might be done by those with other motives and objectives."

"I'm trying to do just that, but events may end up forcing our hand."

"Our surest weapon is the truth!" added the scholar-priest.

"Until we arrive at a point where even that doesn't matter anymore," said the bishop.

CHAPTER 12

The first thing the bishop did on Monday morning was to clear the courtroom. This, of course, had no effect on the boisterous crowds that had gathered in the square outside, except to provide the added incendiary fuel of uncertainty.

Safely inside, the nervous prosecutor, Fra Lorenzo, rose in a flutter of flowing robes, his monkish tonsure newly shaved and trimmed, and addressed the court. "My lord and learned judges, I regret to give formal notice of my intention to ask the court to recommend the death penalty for the accused."

Paire Miquel rose to his feet with much less ceremony. "On what grounds, may I ask?"

"A just punishment for the crime of premeditated murder," Lorenzo announced with a certain self-satisfaction in his voice.

"If this be the murder of our beloved curé of Bastanès, I must point out to my esteemed colleague that the accused was not even in the same town at the time of the murder, but was, in fact, safely ensconced in your lordship's own gaol!"

Lorenzo looked annoyed at the truculence of his judicial adversary. "My esteemed colleague well knows that a witch has the power of bilocation, and, besides, thanks to your intercession with his lordship, the accused was free to utter curses and spells and wave them into the air from where she stood."

"So was my learned colleague thus free, but we have not established that he has either the capacity or willingness to do so."

"Does Pater Michaelus wish to imply that I am a witch?" Lorenzo asked with all the theatrical indignation that he could muster.

"I meant only that such an accusation has not been proven against you, nor has it in the case of the accused, unless I am greatly mistaken."

"But I have scores of witnesses who saw these acts with their own eyes! Does Pater Michaelus wish to suggest that they are ALL liars?"

"I wish to suggest that they do not know for sure what it is that they witnessed, nor could any of us know without all the facts."

Bishop Raymond contributed another dimension to the discussion, something that had been troubling him since the previous meeting. "Are either of you suggesting that I authorize a criminal investigation, which would necessitate my turning the case over to a civil court?"

Lorenzo was beginning to get impatient with the bishop. "I am only suggesting that you issue a finding and recommend an appropriate sentence so that a civil court may take up the case if they so wish."

Paire Miquel was not about to back down. "And on what evidence do you suppose that we may base this recommendation?"

"Mme Balterra is a witch, and someone has died as a result of witchcraft," Lorenzo declared as if it were self-evident.

"Which accusation proves which fact? It seems to me that Mme. Balterra could not have committed the murder unless she were a witch, and that Mme. Balterra is found to be a witch because you say she committed this murder. This is circular logic, neither premise of which has been established to be true."

Bishop Raymond was clearing his throat, preparatory to making a ruling on the question, when they were interrupted by the sound of cheers emanating from the courtyard separating the front entrance of the bishop's residence from the squat, Romanesque cathedral. The pounding of hooves and the blare of trumpets managed to reach everyone's ears despite the ambient cheering. The bishop called, unsuccessfully, for order and silence, after which he abandoned any effort to continue and, instead, ambled to the front door of his home to greet the source of all this excitement.

Men on horseback were processing into the square, followed by a long train of foot soldiers, ponderous supply wagons pulled by teams of six horses each, shield and coats-of-arms bearers, squires and pages, men hoisting banners, musicians, brightly colored "jongleurs," and ragged camp followers. The first column of pike-bearers rode in front, clearing a path through the spectators. Then came the knights, high on their stocky war horses, breastplates shining in the rays of the full, morning sun. Next came the infantry, stopping every now and again to demonstrate a quick collapse into a "turtle" formation, protected from arrows on all sides by a "shell" formed by their interlocked shields. Last of all, the camp followers entered the square, looking wary and suspicious, anxious to find new pockets to pick.

One ragged young lady caught the eye of Paire Miquel and the young court recorder at his side. By tilting her head just so and brushing her abundant black hair against the cleft between her breasts revealed by her low-cut bodice, she made her intentions obvious to both of them. The court recorder felt a sudden dryness in his mouth and hot flush in his face.

Paire Miquel recognized the leader of the company, a certain Sir Tederic, formerly of the court of the duke of Aquitaine, in Bordeaux. When the French had seized Aquitaine from the English in the aftermath of the Cathar Wars, Sir Tederic had switched sides and placed himself under the command of the newly appointed count of Toulouse, who was loyal to the French king. People said that his family motto was "Secum Semper Victor" ("Always Side with the Winner").

Just then, the red-haired priest caught sight of a familiar face. A young man in fine clothes for traveling, with a sword at his side and a lute slung over his shoulder. "Brother Bertrand!" he called out all at once, forgetting for a moment the solemnity of the spectacle.

"No one's called me that in a long time," replied the well-dressed man from on top of his warhorse. "I left the religious life well before taking my permanent vows, and I'm now known as Sir Christobol, knight and traveling troubadour!"

"Quite impressive," replied the priest, "and very different from the student of alchemy and astrology that I remember from my days in Bologna."

"Ah, yes, I discovered the world of chivalric codes of behavior and the passionate love ballads that bid us break those vows for the silken hand of a lady love."

"I never took you for a romantic," the priest remarked with a certain admiration mixed with his natural cynicism.

"You know, there's not much difference between the love of God and the love of a beautiful woman. They both make us better people."

"I suppose that a beautiful woman is, after all, the handiwork of God, as are the beauties of nature and the stars that I study. The TRUTH is beautiful, wherever you find it," added the priest.

"That's why I travel so much," admitted Sir Christobol. "I look for nobility and goodness in knighthood because I really believe in the idea, but everywhere I go, in Bordeaux, in Bologna, in Paris, in Toulouse, I see vainglorious thugs victimizing the poor, raping helpless women, drinking, whoring, swearing, all in the name of being the one force that keeps order these days. Since they are the law, they conclude that no law applies to them. No one, other than the knights is in any position to enforce the law. There must be something higher to which we are all accountable, or the strongest, with the best weapons, will always rule over the weaker and more vulnerable. That's why chivalry and the pursuit of God are really one and the same."

"Even though you have the immediate reward of your lady?" remarked the priest.

"The sweetness of my lady's face is the image of God Himself," said the knight.

"Until the lady's father or brother catches up with you," added the priest.

CHAPTER 13

They would have continued to discuss the issues of chivalry, honor, and the pursuit of the good, the beautiful, and the pleasurable, but they were called to order, from atop his mount, by Sir Tederic the Turncoat to receive a new set of orders.

"People of Lescar, I am commanded by his lordship, the count of Toulouse, to place this town under martial law. Accordingly, as of this moment, all movements in and out of Lescar and Bastanès will be subject to military checkpoints placed at all access roads. All use of unauthorized crossings will be severely punished. No weapons of any kind are allowed in either Lescar or Bastanès, except those of the knights and foot soldiers. Both Lescar and Bastanès will be subject to a strict curfew from sundown until sunrise daily, except on market days. Townspeople are to quarter and feed soldiers when asked and to tend to their daily needs. Anyone caught violating the terms of this occupation will be severely punished." Sir Tederic abruptly turned his mount to indicate that he was finished. Then he dismounted and strode toward the bishop's residence.

"Wait here," Paire Miquel said to his troubadour friend, Sir Christobol, and he turned and made for the courtroom to see about the status of his client.

Inside, the bishop hurried back to his chair, together with the other judges, and waited until Fra Lorenzo, Sir Tederic, and Paire Miquel were in place before him. Miquel was the first to speak.

"We thank Sir Tederic and his lordship, the count of Toulouse, for having so swiftly restored order to our little corner of Christendom, and I assure them both of my continuing cooperation and support.

"In furtherance of Sir Tederic's desire to maintain good order, I agree with my lord bishop and my learned colleague Fra Lorenzo that the prisoner remain secluded, under the custody of the Church, until this matter of grave public concern shall have been properly adjudicated."

"My esteemed colleague takes words out of my mouth before allowing me to speak," remarked Lorenzo. "Might not the witch's security from the crowd be best served by turning her over to Sir Tederic for safekeeping...and questioning?"

"I'm afraid I must insist that this case remain a Church matter as long as Fra Lorenzo sees this as an instance of witchcraft," interjected Bishop Raymond, fully aware of what military questioning would entail.

"My charge here is to keep order, not to dispense justice," Sir Tederic replied with a show of magnanimity. "I am inclined for the time being to leave the accused in the bishop's capable hands pending future considerations."

Paire Miquel tried not to show his relief. Strange, he thought, that Tederic would give in on this key point, even though everyone could see that he held the town in his grip. Assuredly, Tederic was planning something else for Lescar that even this gesture could not totally hide.

Sir Tederic suggested that the court postpone further hearings that day to allow time for Lescar to adjust to the new order. Accordingly, the bishop adjourned until the following morning.

The immediate crisis being somewhat under control, Paire Miquel rushed outside to rejoin his friend Sir Christobol, who, he reasoned, might be of some assistance in the furtherance of his case.

Paire Miquel considered that his movements might be somewhat restricted now, unless he was accompanied by the semblance of authority about him. Christobol might be disposed to negotiate the priest's way through checkpoints and even lend a semblance of official business to his activities. This would have the double effect of calming both the guards and potentially hostile witnesses. Furthermore, the knight might be able to conduct investigations for evidence where the priest would be less likely to be permitted entrance. There was also the matter of Sir Christobol's training (as the postulate, Bro. Bertrand) in the properties of plants and medicinal concoctions, which might, indeed, come in handy.

Paire Miquel found his companion, who had just returned from the stables, where he had requested some cool sponging for his tired horse. He was sitting alone, unwilling to join in the early revelry of his fellow knights in the crowded and boisterous taverns in the center of town. Paire Miquel sat next to him on the bench. There was a tavern down the street, the door to which opened suddenly, emitting the sounds of laughter and merriment as well as the form of a young knight, already drunk, stumbling into the street, bottle in hand. "So, it begins," commented the priest, shaking his head at the sight of one of the town's saviors.

"They're rewarding themselves for the long journey from Toulouse," said Sir Christobol as he took in the familiar scene. "They'll get good and drunk. Then they'll grab the nearest waitress or the host's daughter, and they'll have their way with her as if they owned her. The drunker they get, the less particular they are about whom they fuck."

"You won't find that in any book about chivalry, now, will you," added the priest.

"No. Nor do we troubadours celebrate this kind of conquest by force! It's discouraging, the difference between what ought to be and what is. It's as if the whole story of our life is about making compromises and telling the young to do as we say, not as we do."

"That's what I like about the natural sciences and the faith. They both seek after TRUTH in its purest form."

"But one man's truth is another man's heresy, isn't it?"

Paire Miquel considered that statement for a minute. "In the end, there is only one truth, but there's more than one way to arrive at it. We must consider and discard many things in order to get there. God intends us to use our intelligence, or else He would not have gifted us with it."

"Perhaps you're right," admitted the knight-troubadour. "That's why poetry requires both intelligence and passion."

"It's certainly a skill that separates us from beasts," admitted the philosophical priest.

"Except when we choose to be beasts to one another."

Paire Miquel changed the subject. "Why don't you go for a ride with me? I want to check something out in Bastanès, and I may need you to get me through some checkpoints."

"I've got nothing better to do here. Then you can fill me in on the case that has reduced the whole community to such a frenzy."

They both retrieved their horses from the stables and took the approved road out of Lescar and toward Bastanès.

CHAPTER 14

On the way, they discussed many things, including the exciting manuscript which the priest was carrying to his patron in Italy. "Aristotle's unflinching reliance on careful observation will shake the very foundations of the sciences in the years to come," ventured the priest.

"The careful observation of beauty has always been the preoccupation of poetry," retorted his companion.

"For myself," replied the scholar-priest, I can't decide whether you poets favor the experience of actual beauty or the celebration of the ideal. When the actual doesn't measure up to the ideal, you simply enhance it, in your imagination, until it does."

"Why must you spoil the appreciation of beauty with dull philosophy?" protested the troubadour. "Ah well, I suppose I shall rely on your dispassionate analysis, as a counterbalance to my enthusiasm."

They also talked about Paire Manuel's certitude that Teresa Balterra was NOT a witch and about his suspicions concerning Curé Antoine's murder. Sir Christobol laughed when his friend told him about the figs.

"That's not very original, you know. They say that Livia poisoned the emperor Augustus the same way and that Agrippina the Younger did the identical thing to HER husband, the emperor Claudius."

"I guess it was a dangerous job...being an emperor," mused the priest.

"Being a husband!" rejoined the troubadour, unable to suppress a laugh.

"You're right about one thing, though," the priest said in all seriousness. Poison is historically the preferred murder weapon of females, although my suspicions right now are resting more on a man."

"Your problem is finding a motive. Who would want to kill a village priest in the first place, and who in the world would profit from his death?"

"Exactly," admitted Paire Miquel. "Now, Malin, the blacksmith, was angry with the priest for having secretly arranged the marriage of his daughter, depriving Malin of one of his victims. We know that the blacksmith was prone to cruelty, especially towards those unable or unwilling to defend themselves, like the priest. But those acts were usually unpremeditated drunken, physical outbursts, and his violence never ended in someone's death before. This murder was carefully planned and executed in front of witnesses, who were expected to believe something else about it. This murderer got out unobserved, while everybody was looking the wrong way."

"A puzzling case to be sure," concluded Sir Christobol, "but the predictable direction of suspicion is directly related to the conclusion about whether or not Mme Balterra is a witch."

"You're right, of course. The two problems are inseparable, and the link, if there is one, entirely escapes me. But that's enough about my problems. Tell me about what you've been doing with yourself since leaving the monastery. How does one make a living as a knight and a troubadour?"

"Well," began Sir Christobol, "a knight is in the service of some lord who is in constant need of an army to maintain control over his domain. So, a knight's first duty to his lord is fulfilled by his retention of other men at arms, mercenaries, whom he is prepared to reward with lands and riches. With no other training or trade, I hired myself out as a mercenary, honed my skills as a matter of self-preservation, and ended up in the service of Sir Tederic, who, at that time, was in the service of the duke of Aquitaine. His court was in Bordeaux, and in keeping with his great-grandmother, Aliénor of Aquitaine, that court was the finest example of chivalry, music, and poetry in all of Europe.

Paire Miquel volunteered a compassionate grin. "Bordeaux wine isn't bad, either."

"No, indeed, and I discovered that I possessed a hidden talent for songs and courtly poetry, which was greatly prized there. I learned to play the lute and the hammer dulcimer, and before long, I was honored with a knighthood and the title of troubadour. Then, when Bordeaux was seized by the French and Sir Tederic switched sides, I, who was oathbound to Sir Tederic, switched sides, too, and came to reside and sing my songs in the court of the count of Toulouse."

"A long way from the quiet of the monastery," the amused priest observed without the slightest trace of criticism.

"We all praise God and create beauty in our way, I suppose," the knight-troubadour said in an unnecessary effort to justify himself. "Poetry and music are often used to praise God and lift the hearts of worshipers to the glory of something greater than themselves."

"And to lift the hearts of lovers, I imagine," observed the priest. "Can you give us an example of one of your uplifting songs?"

"It was precisely for that purpose that I brought my lute as well as my sword," admitted Sir Christobol. "Here's an example of something I wrote, myself." Without further encouragement, he hefted his instrument, tightened its strings, and began:

When first we viewed the break of day,
We hid, lest someone spy thy face.
Now, bolder grow we, by thy grace,
And to the world, our love display.
I care not if the world should judge
If we be pure or true or chaste.
Our time is much too brief to waste
By bending to another's grudge!

So, let's away at break of day
And cast our cares upon the breeze
And, like the sunflowers, take our ease
'Til yet again we find our way!

The trees in spring, a lighter green,
Illume our path through wood and dale.
Thine eyes are bright beneath the veil
As, close to you, I dare to lean!
Is this a flame upon thy cheek

That my nearness does ignite?
Oh, please do not depart in fright
When only pleasure I would seek.

So, let's away at break of day
And cast our cares upon the breeze
And, like the sunflowers, take our ease
'Til yet again we find our way!

I bid you stay, oh flower of day,
So sweet and fragrant is thy breath!
For you, I'd tarry to my death
If only thou, with me, will stay.
My hand in thine, and thine in mine,
Together let us always be,
Two hearts, one soul, and finally free,
Our bodies, thus, to intertwine.

So, let's away at break of day
And cast our cares upon the breeze
And, like the sunflowers, take our ease
'Til yet again we find our way!

I see thee always in the trees
When autumn winds the leaves have shorn,
And for thy absence, still I mourn,
Away from me like coldest breeze.
Come back to me just one more time
And let me stroke thy silken hair
Then kiss thee softly, if I dare,
And sing thee yet another rhyme.

So, let's away at break of day
And cast our cares upon the breeze
And, like the sunflowers, take our ease
'Til yet again we find our way!

"That was delightful, my friend! Did you write it for a specific young lady?" the priest asked in genuine admiration.

"She was a countess, the only daughter of a very important retainer at Bordeaux. We planned to marry, but alas, her father disapproved of me, not having been born into the same level of nobility. We parted company under threat of my life and her disinheritance, and shortly thereafter I left Bordeaux with Tederic the Turncoat. A few months later, I heard from a friend that she had married the duchess's older brother and was expecting either his first child or mine. I guess I'll never know which. I really hope the baby takes after its mother! She is probably the most beautiful woman I have ever known. Now all I have is this song to remind me of her."

"Fascinating story," replied the priest. "You should consider putting it to verse as a knightly romance, being careful to change the names, of course."

"Maybe I shall," mused Christobol with a faraway look. "I shall bestow immortality upon Clotilde and her child."

"And you, while you're at it, tell the real story," added the priest, amused at the thought that his friend had undoubtedly already taken great liberties with the truth.

They rode on in silence for several miles, thinking about the confidences they had shared. After surmounting a long curve, they found themselves at the base of the massive shoulder of a mountain, which ancient seismic activity had thrown up in their path. Through the rock face, dividing it almost in half, was a long fissure, like a seam, out of the corner of which cascaded a ribbon of water, fresh, cool, and inviting as it pooled in the rocks below. Instinctively, as if drawn by some unseen benevolence, the two men cantered in the direction of the pool to water their horses…and themselves.

While passing almost directly under the waterfall, Christobol and Paire Miquel caught sight of a massive ribbon of color, resplendent in all its hues, reaching out from the cascade to the sky beyond. Depending on their vantage point of observation, the many-colored ribbon acquired a kind of faint reflection of itself just below it, but then the reflection would immediately disappear as soon as they moved closer.

They stopped to admire the rainbow effect, and Christobol broke the silence to extemporize about the spectacle in verse.

The God of light extends his smile
Upon the sky, a fresco clear.
And with its purity to cheer
The hearts of men who stay a while.
Oh! That we may but take our rest
And bide here longer 'neath this crown.
'Tis more than wealth and great renown
To feel thy glory as thy guest!

So, send away our trials and tasks,
The more to be thy faithful sons.
Hold fast, in time, for such precious ones,
Such jewels, we know not how to ask.

Paire Miquel's reaction, however, was quite different. "I once journeyed to the deserts and arid plains of Africa and encountered a people who called themselves Tuareg. They worshipped the rain as if their prayers would make it linger. When the rainy season did come, they collected the water in cisterns at the feet of rocky outcrops, into which the rain cascaded as if poured from a pitcher. They would dance around the cascades until they saw double rainbows, two ribbons of color, making a complete oval. These were and are rare phenomena, and the Tuareg people took them as a sign that the rain god would grant them sufficient water storage for the year. It was an incredible sight, which I had to experience to believe. I have been trying various optical experiments with prisms since then to duplicate the effect. This is the closest I've gotten to seeing it in Europe."

"I take it that you have written about your experiments to the pope and to the emperor."

"I have," answered the scholar-priest, "and people accused me of making colors by magic. I suppose natural science does seem like magic to those who don't understand it! But in the end, those who seek the truth about what God has created seek the truth about God, and it's wonderful. It's beautiful.

"Magic is illusion and trickery, that which appears to be true and isn't. Both natural philosophy and sacred mysteries are things that appear NOT to be true but ARE. The distinction, to me, is clear."

Sir Christobol granted the point. "I suppose you're right, my friend, but I prefer the pleasures of the senses to those of the mind. Why would you spoil a perfectly beautiful and pleasant experience by trying to explain how it is done?"

"Because" replied the scholar-priest, "causality, proved by being able to duplicate the phenomenon, is part of a larger picture of understanding which gives this physical reality organic unity and meaning. I personally find that very exciting and satisfying."

"As long as you have the pope or the emperor to give you a working space and pay for all the equipment you need. What do you do in this God-forsaken, remote backwater to support yourself in your studies?"

"Oh, the abbot at Sauvelade is himself a learned man, and he had no hesitation about giving me the space at his abbey and using his monastic network to help me find the things I required. He considered it a good idea to bring a little culture to this war-ravaged region."

Sir Christobol approved of his friend's having found a way to work without the pressure of notoriety and expectations. "Still, it's a long way from the center of things."

Paire Miquel became pensive. "I've always tried to be careful and not overstay my welcome in a place such as Rome. I realized that even the pope won't live forever, and there's a limit to his ability to protect me from my enemies. Still, I've been very lucky regarding powerful patronage. Pope Honorius wanted to give me a bishopric in Ireland, but that was a little too far to go for some quiet study. Honorius remains an admirer of my work and has proved himself a champion of both reform and the academic freedom of the masters at the University of Paris. He offered the Left Bank scholars his personal patronage and freed them, by charter, from both the local ecclesiastical and civil authorities. So, you see, we scholars have friends in high places."

"But not in my case," Sir Christobol added as a cautionary note. "Remember, it was your friend the pope who instituted the Holy Office of the Inquisition!"

"Yes, but his intention was to provide an organized and fair process to inquire for the purpose of giving instruction, not punishment. Others, princes and prelates, saw it as a tool for maintaining and expanding control. So much for good intentions!"

"Which brings me to the question of your intentions. Why did you bring me on this trip, really?"

The priest decided to come clean with his friend. "For two reasons, actually. First of all, I may need your protection as I intend to question a man known to be subject to bouts of violence and who most recently expelled me from his property. Secondly, there's someone in Bastanès I'd like you to meet, a silent victim in all this witchcraft business. There may come a time when he will need your help more than mine."

" You mean Mme. Balterra's son? Sir Tederic spoke of a wild boy who was somehow involved. I was wondering what he could tell us about all this."

"Not much, I'm afraid, but at this point, I'm concerned with what will happen to him, depending on how the trial goes." The priest seemed genuinely concerned that things might not end well.

"Enough said. You introduce me to the boy, and I'll make it my business to look after him if the military contingent should remain in the area."

They rode on in silence for a while until they approached the outskirts of Bastanès. Then, having been waved through the checkpoint, they wheeled their horses and headed for the blacksmith's shop.

CHAPTER 15

The fire in the forge was low. The priest-scholar and the troubadour-knight shivered as if they had accidentally entered a place that was under an enchantment. The house was dark, shuttered, and empty. No one was in evidence in the shed area surrounding the forge and the bellows, so the two men ventured through the side entrance of the shop to check out the premises. They found only a straw-stuffed, oversized burlap sack that had evidently been used as bedding for someone who had also used a rolled-up, old, and soiled shirt as a pillow.

Moving back outside, they followed the footpath around back to a barn and some other outbuildings, all in a similarly quiet state. Walking towards them from the barn was a thin and confused-looking dog, actively searching for and expecting to find someone who would be willing to feed him. Paire Miquel pulled a hard roll from his sleeve, dropped to his knee, and offered it to the dog, who scarfed it up ravenously.

They entered the barn, where they found the apprentice, Esteve, lying on a cot, holding his aching head and quite unable to get up and greet his visitors. Paire Miquel knelt beside the boy's cot and inquired after his health.

"I feel miserable, Paire, as if someone has just punched me in the stomach and thrown salt water at my face, into my eyes, at the same time."

"Is Malin at home? Did he accost you here in his barn just now?" The priest wore an expression of concern.

"I haven't seen Malin since yesterday morning when he left for the tavern to help himself to a meal and a couple of pints to drown his sorrows. The mistress threw him out, you know. He's been drinking ever since and sleeping it off in the shop."

The priest frowned and thought for a minute. "When did she throw him out?"

"A couple of days ago, when he came back from the market drunk and asked her why she had let the priest get all of his figs first."

"What did she answer?" asked the priest.

"I didn't hear," said the boy, still drowsy and confused. "She was screaming about how it was his fault that she would lose her soul and all, and I can't be sure what all her ranting meant. Anyway, he stumbled out to the shop to sleep it off, and she took off to God knows where and didn't come back until late that night."

"And he hasn't returned to the house since then?"

"No, Paire. He spends the day at the pub, comes home drunk, and spends the night in the shop. Then he gets up the next day and does the same thing."

Paire Miquel furrowed his brow. "Then how did you end up here so sick?"

Esteve sat up in a sudden panic, his eyes fully open. "I swear I had only one! Please don't tell Madame! Please don't let her beat me!"

"Easy, my boy. No one's going to get you into trouble. What did you have only one of?"

The apprentice began breathing more regularly. "There was nothing to do in the shop. Malin was gone all day, so I wandered into the barn and found this bag of figs that someone had discarded. I figured that no one would mind, so I tasted just one. Then I started to feel awfully sick. You don't suppose she'll whip me for it, do you?"

"Don't worry, Esteve," said Paire Miquel, "I'm sure Madame won't mind if Christobol and I borrow the bag of figs for a little while." The priest picked up the bag and handed it to the troubadour. "Oh, and Christobol, kindly avoid slipping one of those in your mouth until we have had a chance to examine them."

Paire Miquel gave Esteve a drink of water from a flask he had secured around his waist. As he tended to the boy, he looked around for anything out of place. "Did you notice anything else while you were examining the place?"

"Not here in the barn," answered the apprentice, "but I did find a curious little bottle out by the compost pile in the back."

"What kind of bottle?" asked the troubadour, still holding the bag that Paire Miquel had handed him.

"An empty one from what I could tell, maybe some kind of medicine or makeup bottle."

Paire Miquel frowned and sent Sir Christobol back to the compost heap to retrieve the object.

As he and Christobol were getting ready to leave, a rider approached at full speed and stopped in front of them. Christobol recognized him as the squire who served one of the more important knights in his company, and he noticed that the rider was as out of breath as his horse. Still gasping, the squire approached Christobol and the priest to deliver his news without delay.

"The bishop's trial is over. The Inquisition has come to town from Toulouse, and they have both taken over the trial from the bishop's jurisdiction and removed Madame Balterra to their own custody. They are constructing a rack to extort from her a speedy confession. So far, she has confessed to nothing, but most of us think it's just a matter of time."

Paire Miquel could hold his tongue no longer. "Where did they take her?"

"To the basement of the old armory constructed during the Cathar Wars. They had my master post a guard outside."

The red-haired priest leaped on his horse and turned toward the troubadour. "Christobol, take your bag of figs and follow me quickly, and whatever you do, don't snack on them. Esteve, give the squire something to eat, and keep an eye out for Malin and his wife."

He turned the head of his mount and galloped back onto the path without even looking to see if Christobol were following him.

CHAPTER 16

The priest and the troubadour traveled without conversation, hour after hour, each lost in thought to which they dared not give utterance. Paire Miquel's face betrayed imaginings of what he knew was awaiting him in Lescar, followed alternatively by a wrenching agony, confusion, fury, and doubt. He felt utterly helpless and all the more convinced that he had to find a way to wedge something into the cogs of this giant wheel to make it stop. "It seems as if the streams are running faster now," he murmured as if to himself. Sir Christobol knew that he was all but invisible to his friend, which meant that he need not mask his own look of utter desperation.

Their horses and their tempers spent, they rounded a bend at the entrance of Lescar, a town covered in a cope of sullen silence as if finding itself suddenly under hostile occupation. Although still several hours from dusk, the streets were already empty as at curfew. Soldiers policed the major thoroughfares, inspecting papers and contents of the rare wagon. A small group of the idle and curious gathered around the guarded entrance to the derelict armory building that had been converted into a prison.

Sir Christobol cleared the way for his red-headed companion, who followed him into the dark quarters within.

Aside from the occasional flaming torch atop some ancient, weathered wall sconce, the warehouse walls were high-ceilinged and shrouded in gloom. After several minutes, during which their eyes accustomed themselves to the pervasive darkness, they both spied a curious hanging object under a sconce at the far end of the room. Paire Miquel led the way toward it, his troubadour friend trailing behind with both curiosity and foreboding.

Upon closer inspection, Paire Miquel noted that the hanging object was human, female, naked, and covered with sweat and grime, evidence of long hours of suffering and deprivation. She was hung like a slab of beef, her wrists secured to ropes, themselves fastened to two overhanging beams. There were sacks of flour tied to her feet to weigh her down and apply additional pressure to her wrists. She had evidently urinated and defecated on the ground beneath her.

"Cut her down!" shouted the priest, beside himself with fury. Quickly he removed his cloak and covered the woman's twitching body.

"Hands off," replied the chief gaoler, seizing the cloak and hurling it to the ground. "This be my prisoner, unless the grand inquisitor says otherwise."

"And I am Madame Balterra's counsel and an officer of the court!" insisted the indignant priest.

"Not of this court, you ain't," replied the gaoler, placing himself menacingly between the priest and his client.

"We'll see about that," said the priest. Although beside himself with rage and helplessness, he appreciated the futility of decking the impudent rogue and getting set upon by six others, who cared little for his clerical status.

"I'll note how well you have come to the defense of the accused," said the gaoler, who had been rather looking forward to a physical confrontation. The priest thought for a moment about indulging him, but then he turned and left.

Paire Miquel headed straight into the bishop's residence, while Christobol waited for him outside, surveying the placement of sentries in different areas. The troubadour noted that there were few remaining in the vicinity of the residence since the removal of the prisoner to the armory. At the same time, he noticed that ordinary people looked away from his glance and were refusing to look him in the face. It was as if he were somehow contaminated by association with the wondering priest-scholar.

Paire Miquel forced himself past the bishop's secretary and into his lordship's private office. The bishop, in a wrinkled cassock, his bald head uncovered and his eyes looking tired and sore, was still poring over legal tomes and papal bulls. His fist landed on the scrap of parchment on the desk before him. "That's it, by God! I've got them dead to rights."

"My lord?" Paire Miquel sought to reassure himself that the bishop was aware of his presence.

"Miquel, my son, how good of you to come and see me. No one's bothered to give me the time of day since the Inquisition poked their sharp noses into my business."

Paire Miquel was surprised by Bishop Raymond's use of the Langue d'Oc, rather than the more formal Latin, to address him. "I just came from the armory. This is an outrage. Treating her like a convicted heretic, hanging her like a side of meat, invoking the name of God and his Church to justify such treatment."

"I found it! In 866, Pope Nicholas I wrote, 'Quasi rem nec divina lex nec humana prosus admittit (Such a thing is totally unacceptable under both divine and human law).'" He continued with the pope's dissertation. "'Since confession should be spontaneous and not forced, it should be proffered voluntarily, not violently extorted... Will you not at least blush for shame and acknowledge how impious your judicial procedure is? Likewise, suppose an accused man is unable to endure such torments and so confesses to a crime he has never committed. Upon whom...will now devolve the full brunt of responsibility for such an enormity, if not upon him who coerced the accused into confessing such lies about himself?'" Bishop Ramond smiled with self-satisfaction. "I have no doubt, I'd have admitted to killing my grandmother if they so much as threatened to torture me like that!"

"I know what you're saying is true, but who is listening to such counsel in these times of power struggle and fanaticism?"

"Listen, Miquel, you must drop this case. You must quit all participation in these proceedings and get out of Lescar and Bastanès as quickly as possible. Get as far away as you can."

"But I can't leave Teresa to be devoured by these vultures. I must do something to save her!"

"Your devotion to duty—or to her—has blinded you, my friend. They wouldn't have convened the Inquisition for an obscure woman whose only offense was providing herbal remedies and mid-wife services. They'll dispatch her without too much fuss at all, leveraging the public hysteria that's been kicked up about this. Then they'll turn to you. They were content to leave the whole thing with me until you showed up. As Brother Lorenzo has said, your reputation as a scientist and a man of learning precedes you. It's you they want, and now they have a way to get at you."

"Yes, I am a student of natural philosophy, but I'm also a man of God."

"You and I know this, Miquel, but it's a little bit much for them to get their small minds around."

"Nevertheless, my answer is unchanged; I cannot leave, for Teresa's sake and for my own soul."

"Then you only have one choice," Bishop Raymond declared like a man who had reached a decision. "You must win. You must prove her innocence. Their whole case against you will be predicated on the fact that you embraced the cause of the evil one by defending a condemned witch. Your only chance lies in proving them wrong about her."

"That's precisely what I'm prepared to do," replied Paire Miquel, his chin locked in grim determination.

CHAPTER 17

Paire Miquel left his new, and unlikely, friend and rejoined Sir Christobol outside. The streets were quiet and mostly deserted. Miquel barked quick, confidential instructions to the troubadour. "Go pick up Aidor, Teresa's son. He's staying with Mme. Senorant. Bring him and the bag of figs to the abbey at Sauvalarde. Father Abbot will prevent anyone from laying hands on either the boy or the evidence for the time being. I'll join you there shortly to perform some experiments on the figs, but first I must go see the grand inquisitor. Oh, and do ask the abbot if the brothers he sent to Toledo have returned with my witness."

• • •

The red-haired priest knew that Bishop Raymond would not be allowed to forego the privilege of housing Pater Alphonsus Maure, O.P., the head of the Inquisition. This time, Paire Miquel elected not to push past the bishop's secretary but to politely petition for an audience with the inquisitor. After a short delay, he was admitted to the bishop's guest quarters and shown to his seat.

Father Alphonsus was a thin, dark-haired man of indeterminant age whose head, freshly tonsured and shaved, crowned the austerity he wore as proudly as his white Dominican habit. A man not given to personal warmth or empathy, he spoke to Paire Miquel as a scholarly man might address a slow student or the village simpleton. He expressed surprise that the red-haired priest looked forward to the continuation of the trial, what with the abundance of evidence so faultlessly pointing in the direction of the accused. Having confided that he hoped to shortly provide a confession, better for the salvation of Mme Balterra's soul and the swift conclusion of the court's time, he wondered whether Paire Miquel perceived any use in further witness testimony.

The red-haired priest declared that he was anticipating more testimony and that he would like to resume as soon as possible. The Inquisitor smiled in the manner of one concealing the presence of vomit in his mouth and said that they could continue hearing testimony the following Monday, today being Friday, if Paire Miquel found that convenient.

"And whom might you call to testify?" Paire Miquel asked in a disinterested manner.

"I am told that Mme. Malin may have some testimony relevant to the murder of the priest," said Alphonsus, not wishing to give any more detail than he had to.

"I shall be here," said Paire Miquel, nodding and assuming the confident voice of an antagonist equal to the task. "And I must insist that you cut my client down and clean her up before you intend to make a public spectacle of her."

"You may not insist on anything, but I will clean her up before presenting her in court."

"Meaning that you plan to have her spend the weekend in that deplorable condition?"

"All the better to encourage a confession, Father!"

"You will pay to God for this deliberate and calculated cruelty!"

"We shall see who will pay, Father. We shall see…"

Paire Miquel left the room and quickly sought the outside air.

He was restless, so he hastened onto his horse and left the dust of the town behind him. His mount snorted and blew billows of smoke along the forest path to the Abbey de Sauvelade. Sir Christobol met him in the monastery courtyard and told him the boy, Aidor, was safe within the Abbey walls so the new judges could not use him as leverage to secure a confession. Brother Felix and his companion had returned from Toledo with a Spanish monk who was able to read Arabic script. Additionally, Christobol had delivered the figs, unmolested, to Miquel's study. They hurried there to perform their chemical analysis.

Sure enough, the tests were positive for the presence of lethal doses of belladonna, deadly nightshade. So much for the effects of a spell. Now

Miquel had confirmation of his supposition about what had killed the priest, but he still didn't know how, when, and by whom the figs had been laced, who might have a motive for killing Curé Antoine, and how the figs had ended up in the possession of M. and Mme. Malin. All he knew for sure was that he was not looking at the effects of witchcraft but at the result of a very human crime.

Miquel threw a puzzled glance at Christobol. "Curé Antoine rescued Malin's daughter from his clutches by agreeing to perform her marriage. The blacksmith was probably not pleased with that. On the other hand, maybe he was, and it was Mme. Malin who had access to the belladonna through her lover. Let us think some more on this and pray that this mystery unravels itself by Monday."

Without another word, they proceeded to the church for vespers, after which they retired for the night, but not before securing the Arabic-lettered book from the abbot's safekeeping so that Miquel might study it further and bring it with him to court on Monday morning.

CHAPTER 18

Miquel's first stop in Lascar on Monday morning was the armory, which now housed the prison and the torture chamber of Mme. Balterra. He found her in a corner, curled in agonizing pain that permitted her neither comfort nor sleep. She had been doused with a bucket of water and covered with a clean, ragged tunic in a rudimentary effort to make her presentable to the court. She looked at him hopelessly, like a child yearning for release but unwilling to take the step offered her for its accomplishment. Paire Miquel was content to see that although they had broken her body, they had not broken her spirit. Realizing how difficult it was for her to speak, he spoke softly and asked her only to listen.

"Theresa, I am so sorry to see you like this! No, no...shush, shush...don't try to speak. I know how they've treated you, and you know, you're the bravest person I have ever met. Listen, I have proof that you had nothing to do with the murder of that priest and that the charges against you are all false. Give me a chance, and I shall win your freedom. Tell them nothing! Don't give them the satisfaction."

Miquel watched as Teresa Balterra slowly rose to a sitting position. Although her hands were still completely useless, she was willing to try to support her weight on her injured feet and ankles. He didn't know how she put up with the pain or where she found the strength, but she stood defiantly, her head held high, her teeth clenched in her determination not to cry out. It was not pride—she was well past that—but a certain grim determination not to be dominated by those who would have her deny the truth for their own unstated purposes. She knew she was right, and that was enough. With great difficulty, she controlled herself enough to speak.

"Aidor...how is my son?"

"The boy is safe, under sanctuary at the abbey." Miquel caught himself in utter awe and admiration for this woman standing alone against overwhelming force, no matter what the consequences. He must do this for her, no matter what the cost to himself. After sharing bread and water with her, he departed to prepare for the coming confrontation.

Outside the armory, he was awakened from his reverie by Sir Christobol, who was waiting for him, together with the squire who had ridden hard, last Friday to warn them of the arrival of the inquisitors. Miquel grasped the reins of his friend's horse and rattled off a set of instructions to both riders.

"Return to the abbey and secure the boy, Aidor, and two extra horses. Conceal yourselves in the forest behind the bishop's residence. I anticipate we'll have need of a quick exit when this is over. Tell Brother Felix to meet me inside the courtroom and to bring Brother Benignus, the Spanish monk, with him. He is to say nothing to ANYONE about the book, here, concealed in my hood.Remember, be inconspicuous and avoid drawing any attention to yourselves. The boy's life may depend on it."

Christobol and his companion rode off, and Paire Miquel proceeded to the antechamber of the bishop's residence to face the inquisitorial court.

· · ·

The grim assembly, the justice seekers and the morbid onlookers, had already begun to gather in the spaces allotted before the raised dais and the row of high-backed chairs that lined one wall beneath a shining window of stained glass. Miquel had just taken his chair when the one opposite him on the aisle was seized by his old adversary Fra Lorenzo, having been chosen to continue his prosecutorial role under the new jurisdiction.

"Good day to you, Pater Michaelus," said the tonsured monk, an ugly sneer forming on his thin lips.

Paire Miquel nodded politely, although he detected a certain contentment in Lorenzo at having the wandering scholar in his sights. Bishop Raymond, looking sullen and ill-tempered, pushed through the door from the residence and proceeded to a seat on the side. At that moment, the inquisitorial judges processed from a side door to the positions of honor on the dais.

They were a row of identically clad Dominican friars, white robes covered by black cloaks. Paire Miquel reminded himself that they were not consciously malicious. Their severity stemmed from a certain level of fanaticism that sought what they perceived as good ends no matter the means they employed. Paire Miquel deemed such a premise, that the ends justify the means, wrong—it always was, and it always would be— regardless of the intentions of the person or persons who fell into this error. This realization afforded Miquel a clarity of mind that, he hoped, might serve him well in these proceedings.

Father Alphonsus, the chief inquisitor, took the central seat, from which he observed the assembled subjects to assure himself that all were present. He looked with approval at the posts occupied by Fra Lorenzo and Paire Miquel. He turned, however, with annoyance to an armed guard who, apparently, acted as the bailiff and demanded to know the whereabouts of the accused, Teresa Balterra. The bailiff left the room and presently reentered with the accused, who insisted on walking into the courtroom, despite the shackles that impeded her and the chains she dragged after her.

"Presenta (Present)," she pronounced clearly while looking the inquisitor squarely in the eye. An ominous silence settled on the court officers and spectators.

CHAPTER 19

Father Alphonsus acknowledged everyone's presence and instructed Fra Lorenzo to call his first witness. Mme Malin was administered the oath, so help her God, and invited to take the witness stand. As Fra Lorenzo invited her to repeat what she had told him before, her eyes refused to meet those of the monk. Her feet shuffled, despite her efforts to control them, and her hands clasped and unclasped at regular intervals.

After considerable prompting, she related how the curé, on that day, had begun shouting and flinging his arms toward imaginary, menacing phantoms he could plainly see before him. He had mumbled curses and torn the crucifix from around his neck, throwing it to the ground and calling out the name of Our Lord in a most condemnatory fashion. She feared to use his precise language, on peril of her own soul. The parish priest had twitched on the ground, spittle dripping from his lips as he clutched his throat and alternately scratched his arms and chest. Then he had rolled his eyes and shaken his head to clear his vision, all the time swearing and screaming. Finally, he had lain still, dead, as the hand of the evil one had pressed the life out of him like a great anvil.

Mme. Malin concluded her testimony in a state of near hysteria, her breathing shallow and rapid. The room fell deathly silent as people absorbed her testimony. Paire Miquel immediately rose to offer her a flask of water to calm her, and, touching her arm gently, he offered her a fig from the bag he had taken in with him as a bit of refreshment for the woman. Immediately her breathing became regular, and she politely demurred.

#yabsticker

you-are-beautiful.com

"Don't you care for figs, Madame?" the red-haired priest asked with all the solicitude he could muster.

"Oh, yes, but I have no need of them right now. Thank you."

"But these came from the Bastanès market. Surely, they would help settle your nerves."

"My lord inquisitor," interrupted Fra Lorenzo. "The witness has already refused the fruit."

"How very biblical of you, Madame. Perhaps we should consider you a new Eve! Or…should I offer some figs to his lordship, the grand inquisitor?"

"No! Don't do that," said Mme. Malin.

"Isn't that because you know what Sir Christobol and I know from having tested them at the abbey, that they are laced with belladonna? Why did you do that, Madame?"

"That's ridiculous, mon paire! Why would I want to poison a priest?"

"Because he wasn't your intended victim, was he? Your real victim was supposed to be your husband, the village blacksmith. He loves figs, doesn't he? Almost as much as he loves drink."

"He used to beat me regularly, every time he had too much to drink."

"So, when you saw the bottle of belladonna in the wagon of your lover, the barber, you thought, why not? He had it coming to him. He loves figs so much he'd even administer it to himself, and you'd take advantage of the witchcraft hysteria to deflect the blame."

Mme. Malin looked like a trapped animal, but she said nothing.

"But that isn't the way it worked out," continued the red-haired priest. "You weren't figuring on the fact that Curé Antoine loved figs, too, and that Malin was already drunk that day. The curé was faster than Malin and got to the fruit stand first. It was the curé who bought up all the figs and couldn't help tasting five or six of them right out of the sack.

"What would you say if I examined the body of Curé Antoine right after the murder and found unmistakable signs of belladonna poisoning on his mouth and fingers and that belladonna poisoning produces the same kind of mad effects as witchcraft and demonic possession? So, you poisoned the priest, didn't you?"

Madame Malin burst into tears. "I didn't mean for anything to happen to the priest. It was all an accident!"

"But your husband knew what you had done. He moved out of your house that very night and started taking his meals at the tavern. He wasn't going to give you a chance to make a second attempt."

"I'm so sorry," she said as they led her off the stand, in the custody of the bailiff. " I had to be free of him. I couldn't take it anymore, I simply couldn't. He deserved to die for what he done to me. He did!"

CHAPTER 20

The murmuring of the crowd threatened to take over the room. "Order, order!" the chief inquisitor shouted to regain control. "There were other concerns, about the crime of witchcraft, which were under consideration before the murder occurred."

"In that regard, my lords, if we have heard from all of Fra Lorenzo's witnesses, I wish to proceed with my own witnesses." Paire Miquel rested his hand on a ponderous volume, which he had been keeping on his person the entire morning.

The inquisitors huddled in conference, after which the chief inquisitor asked Fra Lorenzo, "Have you completed the presentation of your witnesses, Brother?"

The officious monk rose to address the court. "I have, my lords."

Lorenzo resumed his seat, and Miquel rose to address the judges. "Except for the repetition of some idle gossip and speculation, your case revolves around the defendant's possession of a certain offensive text, namely, the contents of this book," said Paire Miquel, holding the volume up for all to see. He handed the book to the chief inquisitor, who refused to even touch the thing, lest he be contaminated by its contents. Failing that offer, Paire Manuel asked Fra Lorenzo to stipulate for the court that this was the book of supposedly heathen origin that Mme. Balterra was accused of using in her chapel for unholy purposes. The prosecutor judged it so, also without taking it into his hands. "I beg the court to call upon a textual expert, Brother Benignus of Toledo, Hispania. Here are papers from his abbot stipulating his academic credentials as an expert on ancient texts."

The inquisitors debated with Fra Lorenzo for some time about the Spaniard's qualifications and what they thought Paire Miquel actually had up his sleeve. Finally, and after many questions posed in Latin directly to the monk about his activities at home, Father Alphonsus agreed to allow him to testify.

Paire Miquel was careful to question his witness in Latin because his native tongue was a form of Catalan, not Langue d'Oc. The red-headed priest asked the monk if he had examined the book in question.

"Sic (That is so)," answered the Spaniard.

"And what sort of book would you say it is?" asked the red-haired priest.

"Well, as you know from having worked in Toledo, Christians, living hundreds of years under Moorish rule, adopted the dress and speech of their conquerors. They even used the Arabic alphabet and produced works such as this one, which is actually a transliteration of Latin words represented phonetically by Arabic letters."

"So, you mean that this book is actually in Latin and anyone who knows how to pronounce Arabic letters can decipher it?"

The Spaniard was quick to demystify the process. "This practice was fairly common in what used to be Al-Andalus (Moorish Spain)."

"I see," said Paire Miquel. "Would you care to read for us the opening pages of the book?"

The Spaniard took the book from Paire Miquel's hands and opened it to the first page of text. There was much murmuring and the stopping of ears before the witness was permitted to go forward. He cleared his throat and raised his voice so that all might hear.

In principio erat Verbum et Verbum erat apud Deum et Deus erat Verbum. Hoc erat in principium aput Deum. Omnia per Ipsum facta sunt, et sine Ipso factum est nihil quod factum est.	In the beginning was the Word, and the Word was with God, and the Word was God. He was in the beginning with God. All things were made by Him, and without Him was made nothing that was made.

The Spaniard stopped reading because of the murmuring and because the inquisitors were discussing among themselves what, if anything, remained of the charge against Mme. Balterra.

Paire Miquel turned to the panel of inquisitors. "Do my lord inquisitors require further explanation concerning this particular text?" He was met with hesitant, dumbfounded silence.

He swung around to his witness. "Brother Benignus, in your expert, scholarly opinion, is this a heathen text inspired by the devil?"

"Absolutely not. This is the Gospel of our Lord according to St. John, transliterated into Arabic characters but clearly and phonetically Latin in its content."

The red-haired priest looked at the grand inquisitor with a triumphant smile on his face, but the inquisitors were deep in consultation about where to go from here.

The level of murmuring in the courtroom was rising to a deafening pitch, so much so that the sounds from the gathering crowd outside the bishop's residence was partially blocked out. Soon angry voices, from outside, began to intrude on the confusion that reigned within, and people in the courtroom became aware of the mounting dissidence between the mood within the courtroom and the mood without.

Word was beginning to spread among the gathering populous that the progress of the case was moving in Teresa Balterra's favor. Notwithstanding what everyone knew for a certainty, the rumor was that the Inquisition had already acquitted the hapless woman of murder and were about to acquit her of witchcraft! The mood of the crowd grew angrier as their numbers swelled.

As if in reaction to the rising tempo of a drumbeat, people jostled one another in elevated excitement. Breathing became rapid and short, and eyes darted nervously from one side of the square to the other. Restless spectators raised lit torches into the air, and the impatient farmers raised their pitchforks like pikes, making threatening grunts as they did so.

Louder and louder, the murmuring rose, until audible protest replaced the insistent whispering with which the information about the trial had begun to spread. Justice, they said, must be the verdict of the court, or justice would be the prize that they would wrench, as a body, from the witch's torn garments.

Esteve, the blacksmith's apprentice, slipped through the crowd and into the building to report to Paire Miquel what was happening outside. "I don't know precisely when things got to this point, but the mood of the crowd has definitely turned ugly. They're snarling and baying for blood."

The priest-scholar furrowed his brow. He knew they were well beyond the point of susceptibility to reason. "How long do you think we've got until they overwhelm the guards and push in here?"

"Only a few minutes at best," replied the frightened boy.

At that moment, a hand tapped Paire Miquel on the shoulder. He turned to meet the eyes of Bishop Ramond, who cautioned Miquel with a finger to his lips.

Rising to his feet, Paire Miquel asked the court if it was prepared to render a verdict in the case of Mme. Balterra. The inquisitors eyed each other with uncertainty while listening to the raucous riot set to explode at any moment.

Finally, the Grand Inquisitor rose to his feet and signaled for some semblance of silence. Looking scornfully at all the room before him and with raised voice, he declared, "As none of the unruly hooligans who call themselves members of this community have displayed the least consideration for the careful judgment and justice of this court, we deny you a verdict and release Mme. Balterra to your own resources. Deal with her and her spokesman as you will." The inquisitors declared the session at an end and looked around for an avenue of exit and escape.

Pandemonium broke out in the room, with people looking for either routes of escape or places to hide until tempers had been allowed to lower. Bishop Raymond seized Paire Miquel's arm and asked him to pull Mme. Balterra, still unsteady on her feet, after them and toward a side door behind the last chair on the dais. While everyone was looking for a way out, he was offering a way in. This turned out to be a little-used passageway to the bishop's private quarters. Once there, he stuffed some bread, a skin of water, and a purse containing three thousand florins into the sleeve of Miquel's robe and led them through a secret panel in the wall to a passage that emptied into a forest clearing that lay fifty or sixty paces behind the residence.

On the other side of the clearing, Miquel caught sight of Christobol, Aidor, and the horses, concealed in a clump of trees. Christobol pointed to one of the horses and pantomimed that he had remembered to pack the Aristotle manuscript, without which he was sure that Miquel would be unwilling to depart. Before rushing to his party, the priest turned to Bishop Raymond and placed his hand on the older man's shoulder. "Why did you decide to help us? I do not wish to seem disingenuous, but I'm definitely curious.

"Well, first of all, you convinced me that she is completely innocent. And secondly, you reminded me why I became a priest in the first place, and I'll never be able to thank you enough for that."

"God be with you, my lord," he said while offering his arm to the woman.

"Farewell, my friends," the bishop said to the ragged-looking company before him. "I'll say I saw you go the other way, towards Spain. That might give you a little bit of a head start."

The old man hurried back inside of his house.

CHAPTER 21

Sir Christobol took the lead while Aidor stayed back to accompany his mother and Paire Miquel brought up the rear. Teresa was in no condition for either long or strenuous travel, so they established a moderate pace, intending to reach the small Benedictine house at Tarbes by nightfall.

Christobol had purchased some clothes from Mme. Senorant, who had been looking after Aidor while his mother was in prison. When the sun was high, they stopped at a running stream and invited Teresa to bathe and change into the clothes purchased by a man sensitive neither to fashion nor to the concept of size. The men stayed, with their backs to her, until she had emerged, dressed.

The transformation was dramatic. Her olive skin glistened in the sunlight, and her hair, loose to her waist, shone with a thickness and luxuriousness that contrasted sharply with the matted rat's nest to which they had, up to this point, become accustomed. She stood, her muscles having experienced a certain amount of temporary relief, with a newfound grace and composure, her long neck lifted above her shoulders and her hand resting on her hip. She clearly was, both men surprised themselves to admit, a woman more attractive in freedom than she had been in captivity. She was still not the image of the high-born maiden that Sir Christobol would have pursued against father and family and immortalized in his verse, but Paire Miquel indulged himself with thoughts he would not have consciously acknowledged only hours before.

Teresa felt refreshed, and she suggested they ride on in lieu of taking their midday break. So, they mounted and continued, Miquel careful to keep his eyes averted from Teresa. While keeping careful watch for any signs of imminent pursuit, they continued through the forest in silence.

At last, they spied a small stone structure atop an outcropping of rock, on the top of which was an old and weather-worn cross. They mounted a path, the many turns of which brought them to the open northern gate of a monastic establishment in the wilderness. The abbot at Sauvalade, they learned, had sent a rider ahead with a message requesting that these guests be granted sanctuary. Accordingly, the rector of St. Gilles at Tarbes stood at the gate, ready and anxious to meet them and offer them lodging and refreshment. After some rest and repose, they joined the monks for vespers and what they agreed was a sumptuous dinner. Then a young brother showed them to their rooms and informed them that they would meet with Father Abbot after Laudes and Holy Mass in the morning.

• • •

"So, you've escaped the Holy Inquisition, have you?" said Abbot Laurent when Brother Anselm left them at the abbot's office door. "More power to you, I'm sure. You know they've completely lost sight of their original purpose."

"And it didn't take the civil authorities long to figure out how to use the unhinged authority of the Church to further their own ends," added Paire Miquel, happy to have found a sympathetic auditor.

"What are your plans now?"

"We want to reach Italy, either the Papal States or the territory loyal to the emperor, where we might expect to find protection and patronage."

"Then I suggest you choose quickly between them. Rumor is that they are not on particularly good terms these days."

"They both have the highest regard for mathematics, astronomy, and medicine," observed Paire Manuel.

"Yes, but not as much respect as they have for the security of their borders. Between his base in Naples and Sicily and his territories in Germany, Romagna, and now Tuscany, the emperor has the pope basically surrounded. His Holiness is just a little uncomfortable with the arrangement."

"You don't seem to have much trouble getting the news out here in the wilderness," commented Miquel.

"Oh, news is really very slow around here. We had hardly gotten word about the emperor's excommunication when he seemed to be back in the pope's good graces, with a pledge to go on a crusade. Events are so changeable!"

"Well, for us, getting away from here is our priority."

"So I gather," replied the abbot. "Listen, there's a string of monasteries between here and Umbria, and I can give you letters addressed to each of them to assure your safety until you can make your own arrangements. I'd be happy to do so."

"Thank you, Father. We are truly indebted to you."

"Don't mention it, my friend. You would do it for me if our roles were reversed. Feel free to stay here as long as you want while Madame recovers."

"I think we'll pack something to eat on the road and get going. I don't know if they plan on pursuing us all the way to Carcassonne."

"I'll have Brother Anselm prepare something for you while you get your mounts loaded up and I get busy on those letters."

The four travelers prepared for their departure.

CHAPTER 22

Abbot Laurent had warned them to stick to the forest paths in lieu of the main roads, which meant that their ability to survey the surrounding area for suspicious riders was limited. That also meant, of course, that they were less visible to potential pursuers, an offsetting advantage.

"I don't know what you're so worried about," Christobol said from his lead position. He turned his neck and torso to address the riders following him. "The lady has already been released by the Inquisition. Why would they pursue anew?"

"Because Teresa is not their true object. I defied the Inquisition. I'm the one they want to bring to justice," Paire Miquel replied in a thoughtful, calculating tone. For the first time, he considered he might be endangering the party by his very presence. Even if he were to take refuge in some monastery or another, Sir Tederic and his men would believe that he was still with the party, and his disappointment upon learning that the scholar-priest had slipped through his fingers would cost his friends their lives. No, he must somehow get them to safety first. At least, that's what he told himself.

The winding path they followed through the forest was covered with overgrowth and tangled roots. Tree branches hung low, shrouding their progress in ominous, perpetual twilight. They found it necessary to continually dip and weave to avoid the lowest branches. The sound of birds, insects and scurrying animals put them all on edge.

To provide some relief from the rising tension of watchfulness, Sir Christobol pulled out his lute and composed a song to provide some momentary distraction:

Our woodlands speak an ageless song,
Before the first of men arrived.
She cries of timeless epochs, long
Before the first of seasons thrived,

When towering trees did ever rule
From leafy heights to mossy bed
And furtive beasts 'gainst Nature cruel
Did forage food so young were fed.

Oh, that I could have slept within
The gentle folds of leafy moss,
To suck the breasts of saplings thin
And care for neither gain nor loss.

But now our passage must be swift
Before more huntsmen find us here.
No more in streams to careless drift
May we surrender out of fear.

On, on, forever striving,
Past our dreams, our friends surviving.

"Dreams," thought Paire Miquel, as if Christobol's poem had actually emanated from his own wayward thoughts. Abruptly, his mount came to a halt. All he could see was the silhouette of the lady he had rescued riding in stark profile on her mount. Teresa, Aidor, and Miquel halted, and after a few steps, so did Christobol. They exchanged a quiet glance. The song did not lighten their spirits, but it suspended their watchfulness so they could listen to the benign voices all around them. Teresa was aware that Miquel was watching her, to the exclusion of all else, and if he could have seen the expression of longing, instead of the outline and shaded interior of her silhouette, Miquel would have been unable to mask his own, reciprocal feelings.

When they faced front, they caught sight of the tiny village of Saint-Girons, nestled around the walls of a tenth-century monastery of that name. Since it was nearly dusk, they decided to break their journey here for the night.

The next day, after Prime, they recommenced their flight, this time intending to reach the town of Béziers. At the mention of the name, the monks were alarmed.

The northern barons still maintained a garrison there from Toulouse. It was said that during the Cathar wars, the residents of Béziers were so resentful of the heavy-handedness of the northerners that the Cathars and Catholics banded together to defend the town. When the northerners eventual overwhelmed them, the invaders systematically slaughtered Catholic and Cathar alike, man, woman, and child, to the tune of some twenty thousand souls. They burned down the cathedral, whose roof collapsed, killing everyone who had been seeking sanctuary inside. The lingering resentment resulting from the massacre necessitated the maintenance of knights and foot soldiers to ensure order (and compliance).

The monks urged Paire Miquel to cut south to Limoux and then follow the Mediterranean seacoast to Aigues Mortes, avoiding both Carcassonne and Béziers. Teresa and Christobol quickly agreed to that plan.

The route south was far less traveled this far from a major seaport, and they had the advantage of flatter terrain, which was a good deal easier on the horses. This was preferable now because speed was of the essence. They had always been wary of Sir Teneric's pursuit from the west, but now a sortie from Carcassonne to the north, and Béziers, from the east, would secure them in a trap, with their backs to the sea. They had to break loose and make it to Aigues Mortes.

By midday, they had reached the outskirts of Limoux, where they found refreshment for their horses and themselves on the banks of the River Aude. It was Market Day, and the narrow streets of the Vielle Ville were crowded with vendor stands, tasting booths, and the laughter of children enjoying a day off from the fields. So many visitors from neighboring villages and farms were in evidence that the company felt little anxiety about standing out. In fact, Teresa would have liked to stay and, perhaps, purchase cloth for making better-fitting garments, but Paire

Miquel warned them that they could not afford to delay. At that moment, they realized that Aidor was no longer with them.

Teresa covered her mouth with her hand to suppress a startled cry. Christobol ran to the end of the street to give himself a better view of the booths beyond that point. Paire Miquel began pushing people aside to peer into gathering pockets of milling spectators. Had someone seized the boy to use as leverage to secure Miquel without a fight, or had he simply wandered off in pursuit of some amusement? He'd certainly not been at liberty to amuse himself for the last several days. Miquel caught the eye of a stranger giving him a momentary glance of interest. Teresa couldn't help looking panicky, as the crowd suddenly seemed to be circling closer around her.

Presently Paire Miquel emerged from a small gathering, towing Aidor by his upper arm. In one hand, the boy still held a piece of candied fruit he had been sampling when the scholar-priest had apprehended him.

"Young man, where have you been?" asked Teresa, tears of joy in her eyes.

"I just made a stop at a stand where a girl was giving away some free samples," replied the boy.

"I know this hasn't been much fun for you, but our lives depend on our being together and our being strong. Your mother is alive, and I want to keep it that way." Both Paire Miquel's hands were on Aidor's shoulders, and he held eye contact long enough for the boy to realize in how much danger they all were. The chastened lad was handed the reins of his horse, and then they all mounted and rode away.

The scene occurred under the eye of the very same stranger whom Paire Miquel had observed during their search for the boy. This time, the stranger concealed himself behind a display of knitted blankets at a nearby stall. As the Bastanès company rode away, Paire Miquel turned in his saddle long enough to notice the stranger emerge from his hiding place and note the direction the company had taken.

CHAPTER 23

The next leg of their journey brought them very close to Béziers, but they were careful not to take the road into town. They were joined, however, by travelers who were leaving for their return journey home. The four refugees from Bastanès took comfort in the company, as the presence of witnesses tended to discourage the harassment of fellow travelers. Their pace slowed, and they actually exchanged smiles and pleasantries with their newfound companions.

The further they advanced away from Beziérs, the fewer travelers remained, and the more they were conscious of losing their anonymity. The terrain, too, grew more constricting and dangerous as the forest to their right thinned and became an expanse of swampland into which they dared not enter for fear that their horses might lose their footing and throw them into the soggy, muddy bottom. The path on which they were forced to remain turned into a road that was clearly visible from all directions. The changing landscape offered them no alternative routes where they might find shelter from prying eyes.

Sir Christobol offered to ride ahead to scout out the area while the company continued its progress. No sooner had he returned with the all-clear than the company approached a wagon in the road just ahead, its back wheels evidently caught in a muddy patch. The accident must have just happened, because Christobol had passed this way minutes before and had not stopped to help.

Paire Miquel drew up to Teresa and Aidor and greeted the man who was trying to wedge a tree branch under one of the wagon's sunken rear wheels.

"Good day, sir. Might we be of some assistance to you?"

"I'd be grateful if you would lend your back to lift the rear of this cart long enough for me to slip this branch beneath it."

"Ay, that I can do," the priest said as he dismounted and moved toward the wagon.

When Aidor moved to give Paire Miquel a hand, two men suddenly jumped from their concealment behind a bush. They were brandishing swords and tree-branch clubs, screaming at the company like wild men. The priest recognized the lead assailant as the observer with whom he had locked eyes in Limoux. Fortunately, they were all on foot.

"Flee, Teresa!" he shouted since he had the presence of mind to notice that the woman was still on her mount. The woman, however, held her ground, determined as she was to never permit anyone to terrorize her again.

Miquel drew his sword, parried the head man's downward blow, and delivered a kick to the stomach of his opponent that was hard enough to throw him off his feet. Another of the assailants took a swing at him, but Paire Miquel turned and skewered the man with the end of his sword.

Finally, Teresa turned and galloped away. Miquel was momentarily distracted by her movement, and the recovered leader raised his arm to slice the priest's skull, but then, Aidor struck the assailant with a large branch, sending him crumbling to the ground. A horse leaped from concealment and pursued the fleeing woman. The lightly armored rider was none other than Teneric the Turncoat, intent on the most vulnerable of his prey.

At that instant, a horse jumped to clear the stationary wagon and took off in pursuit of Sir Teneric. It was Christobol, who had seized one of the wagon horses nearer to him than his own and turned in pursuit. The young man overtook the Turncoat and slapped the rear of Teneric's mount with the blunt end of his sword. The startled animal reared, but the experienced master quickly maneuvered to control him. Nevertheless, Christobol had purchased enough time to secure himself a high-ground position from which to better control the fight. Teneric, infuriated by the young man's boldness, charged up the small embankment that separated him from his adversary.

Both men parried blows with equal ferocity until Christobol succeeded in maneuvering his opponent off the road and into the swamp.

With one additional step, Teneric's mount sank into the soft earth, lost his balance, and threw his rider into the muddy water. The weight of the rider had ensured that the horse would suffer a broken leg and become useless.

Teneric lay still in the mud and water, furious beyond words. Christobol stood over him, his sword poised at the Turncoat's neck until, according to the convention of chivalry, his fallen opponent uttered the words of surrender. The fallen knight regained his composure and glared at the young knight who had bested him. "Reinforcements from Lescar will arrive shortly, you know."

"I doubt that you'll want the recount the tale of having been overcome by a subordinate. Besides, I rather suspect that your masters from Toulouse would rather let this whole matter simmer down than prolong the vendetta."

"One day, our paths will meet again, young traitor, and I assure you that day will be your last."

"So be it," said Christobol, sure that a life like his was not destined to experience old age.

Teneric led his crippled horse off, back up the road, and Christobol returned to his other companions, the lady's horse following behind him. Once he had ascertained that everyone was unhurt, he urged all deliberate speed to someplace safe and secure. "The country around here doesn't afford much cover for weary travelers."

He told them that the road ahead led to a large expanse of salt flats surrounded by marshes. The landscape offered not a single tree behind which to seek concealment, nor were there sources of fresh water for themselves or their animals. The overland journey towards the Var and Milan was mountainous and slow, to say nothing of the presence of the armies of the emperor lending support to the duke of Milan's claim to Nice and its surroundings. Paire Miquel thought that their best chance would take them by sea from the French seaport of Aigues Mortes to Latina, in central Italy, which, at that time, was part of the Papal States. Accordingly, they decided to risk the salt flats to reach Aigues Mortes and the passage to the Mediterranean.

CHAPTER 24

They raced through the salt flats, surrounded by nothing but mud and swamps, the sun beating relentlessly down on the crystal deposits the advancing and receding waters had left. Their eyes squinted against endless fields of white, like snow or a fathomless desert, stretching as far as the eye could see. As the sun sank lower behind them, the salt, by degrees, turned a light-pink hue as if reflecting something unearthly. Suddenly they felt themselves in an alien land that was forever losing itself in the gaping mouth of the sea. Like Odysseus and his crew, they had discovered an enchanted place that even the gods had left behind without a single blessing to sustain it.

"Look," said Teresa, her arm and finger reaching toward the horizon of nothingness. Suddenly, over the hump of the earth came speeding, graceful objects that seemed to ride on the wind and call forth waves of trembling from the ground beneath. The thundering objects grew closer, and Aidor could make out that they were a herd of wild white horses running breathless and free, their snowy manes blowing in the wind like the pennants of kings. Their land was so vast that they took no notice of the passers-by, as if, compared to their princely selves, the travelers were just little specks of no consequence flapping in the wind. The wild beasts regarded the panorama of land like conquering Seljuk Turks stretching the limits of their empire. They were too great and powerful to notice the petty intrusion of mere humans.

After the horses had left and the ground stopped shaking, a flock of unlikely pink birds rose as if from pink eggs in the ground. The travelers had never seen such creatures before, and they remarked at the length of their spindly legs and the elegant curvature of the long necks with which they stretched their beaks to the ground. The swamp was clearly their natural habitat, and their light weight enabled them to walk as if on top of the waters, never faltering or sinking.

Christobol looked as if he were about to burst into verse, but he only managed to exclaim, "What is this place that some jealous god would keep to himself for his own pleasure?" Miquel alone smiled as if he'd seen all this, and more, in his travels but had not lost the capacity for wonder that had seized him in his youth.

As they continued eastward, their eyes peeled for white horses, Aidor spotted a stationary object in the distance. As they drew closer, the object loomed higher on the horizon and became more distinct. It stood like a monolith, alone against a limitless sky. Closer still, they discerned a huge stone tower pointing into the sky like Babel itself.

Paire Miquel explained that the object was a watchtower intended to provide its owner a vantage point from which to survey the surrounding salt fields and waterways. The tower was placed strategically to give early warning in the event of an attack.

"St. Louis, the French king, had originally bought a large tract of land from the Abbey of Psalmody on which to construct a French-controlled port on the Mediterranean and a fortress to defend it. Actually, the Carbonnière Tower was the first to be built so that the workers would be secure while the port and its fortifications were being completed. But the property that the monks sold the king was just a mosquito-infested marsh whose waters were too shallow for a seagoing ship to make it in or out, so the king ordered an engineer to design a complex system of canals and dikes to provide dry roadways and a deep channel to the open sea. It was quite a project."

"How did he attract workers there to service the ships?" asked Teresa.

"Well, the laborers who harvested the salt were already there, and he exempted them from the salt tax so that there would be no shortage of workers in the area despite the unpleasant climate. Today the town is thriving, and the port is kept busy in war and in peacetime."

"Do you suppose anybody has spotted us yet?" asked Christobol,

"Probably," speculated the scholar-priest, "but we're far enough from Bastanès and Lescar that it's unlikely that anybody has heard our story, and four riders are hardly an invading army. I don't think anybody would be likely to pay us any notice."

"Good," said Aidor, "because I see the walled town in front of us."

The entire town was encircled by a thick stone wall, its turrets looming above them. Armed guards wore bored expressions as they gazed at the monotony of the bare wasteland that stretched out endlessly in all directions. Wagons clattered on the cobblestone path that led to the gate, a peculiar contraption that opened from top to bottom. With its system of chains and pulleys, the whole spectacle looked like the open mouth of a giant, thirsty beast.

"With all these wetlands surrounding us, it's ironic that the one item in short supply is fresh water. I hear they had to dig a channel all the way to the Rhone to bring it in," reflected Paire Miquel.

Aidor turned in his saddle, a puzzled expression on his face. "What does 'Aigues Mortes' mean in their language?"

"It means 'Dead Waters,'" replied Teresa, a worried expression on her face.

"A reference to the stagnant swamps, I presume," said the scholar-priest. "We only need to stay here long enough to secure passage on a boat to Latina. Then we will be beyond the reach of anyone who would do us harm."

The company proceeded through the town center, past the markets and entertainments that catered to sailors as well as the local laborers. A merchant offered to sell Christobol a bottle of his homemade wine to quench his traveler's thirst, while a woman with three missing front teeth offered to give Paire Miquel a moment of passion in exchange for a silver piece. Christobol, it seemed, could not resist, while Miquel excused himself from entering into such a transaction. Aidor expressed a particular interest in what the woman might be selling before Teresa seized him firmly by the shoulder and pulled him away.

After taking some rest and following a repast of barley bread, pomegranates, and wine, the company turned right, toward one of the estuaries that formed the veins and arteries of the town. Their banks were piled high with cargo destined to be loaded onto seagoing ships. All the while, Paire Miquel was careful to leave a distance between himself and Mme. Balterra, and he assiduously avoided engaging her in conversation.

They walked the canals, looking for a captain, one headed for the Italian coast and willing to take on four passengers without asking very many questions. At last, they encountered a tall and lanky sailor who was taking a break from supervising the loading of salt barrels into a respectable looking balinger. Her one square sail was nearly furled to the yardarms, and her oars were stores neatly on deck.

The captain introduced himself as Isnardon. "The *Marie-Pierre* is a good-sized craft, twelve oars, a full load of cargo in the hold, plus passengers. Good speed."

With no multi-deck structures, fore or aft, she looked more like a barge than a seagoing vessel in Paire Miquel's view. She was, nevertheless, sturdy enough and had canvas sheets stretched onto four poles to serve as protection on deck for the passengers. "Where are ye headed?" the scholar-priest asked in as close to the local vernacular as he could get.

"Headed for Terracina, southern side of Latina, on the sea," said Captain Isnardon, his cap pushed back to allow himself to wipe his eyebrow.

"Got room for four more passengers: the lad, the lady, the young man, and me?" asked the priest, wiping his own face with a cloth he kept in the sleeve of his robe.

"You're clearly not traders or growers' representatives, but hell, I don't care none why people want to travel. Pay me in advance, and the only thing I'll hold you to is to be here for the morning tide tomorrow."

Paire Miquel paid him eight hundred florins from Bishop Raymond's purse and assured him they would be on the dock before Lauds tomorrow morning. Having taken care of that business, they made their way to the Abbey of Psalmody to take shelter for the night.

CHAPTER 25

The streets were still dark when the company made its way from the monastery gates to the town and through the labyrinth of narrow passageways along the estuary to Captain Isnardon's mooring. Aidor noted that all the barrels of salt that had been stacked up on the dock had now been securely stowed in the hold of the waiting ship. Sailors were securing lines and double-checking the ship's contents in preparation for departure. The first mate was checking off names from the passenger manifest as each of the prepaid travelers was helped aboard by a crew member. Miquel, Christobol, Teresa, and Aidor, likewise, were checked in and boarded. The crew member who assisted Teresa lingered with his firm grasp around her hand longer than he should have. She tried unsuccessfully to pull away and then glanced at Paire Miquel for help. The priest leaped on deck and grabbed Teresa's hand, securing its release from the crewman. Having accomplished his mission, he led her to another part of the deck and released his grip.

"I trust I have not been too forward, Madame, but it seemed that you required someone to extricate you from a situation you neither invited nor could control."

"Think nothing of it, Paire," replied Teresa, her eyes lowered and quick to look away.

They settled in and made the acquaintance of their fellow passengers, the crew being too busy to fraternize and disinclined to do so, except with Teresa. The passengers included two salt merchants hoping to land a contract for supplying the spice to the entire city of Latina, four Franciscan friars on their way to a provincial chapter meeting in Campobasso, and the four companions from Bastanès, pilgrims headed for Rome to pray before the tomb of St. Peter. None of them used their own names except for the friars, whose names were not the ones given to them at baptism, but the ones they had assumed when they had taken their final vows. They subscribed collectively to the understanding that they would not become overly curious about anyone concerning their true motives for being onboard. Rather, they would accept each other's story as if it were the self-evident truth without resorting to more in-depth questioning. It was not the first time, nor the last, when strangers thrown together on a ship found it safer to play roles and take a holiday from being who they really were in this little microcosm of the world.

At last, they kicked off from the shore, riding the last of the flood tide that temporarily widened and deepened the channel they needed to navigate, to reach the open waters of the Lion Gulf and the Mediterranean Sea. The crew used neither sail nor oars at this stage of the journey. Instead, a seaman stood aft and worked a long pole into the shallow water to inch the ship forward in the passage and, at the same time, measure the depth of the water in which they found themselves. From the bridge, Captain Isnardon carefully watched the poleman as he sounded out the depth, lowering the pole in search of the bottom.

From their covered locations on deck, the passengers could see the sides of the craft coming close to the edge of the channel. Loose grass and seaweed swept against the gunwales like coarse brushes. At the last minute, the ship would steer clear of the port bank, only to move precipitously toward the starboard bank. Teresa thought that the process of managing this channel was very much like threading a needle and, in like manner, required skill and concentration.

Aidor could see small animals and birds running and leaping along the banks to position themselves where they could snap off some young pieces of barnacle protruding from the hull. The birds cried to each other to join the search further downstream. Meanwhile, Christobol, the poet, hung on the starboard gunwale, already motion sick and preparing himself to heave over the side. Teresa offered him a cloth to wipe his forehead, and Paire Miquel produced a skin of water from his sleeve and suggested to his friend that he sip it slowly. Insects buzzed about their ears, and a snake slid into the water from the underbrush on the opposite bank.

Gradually the channel deepened until the poleman could no longer find the bottom. The first mate called for the oarsmen, six on each side, to take over the propulsion. By now, the tide was moving in the other direction, out towards the bay. The channel widened until they smelled different water and felt themselves slicing through the glassy, calm waters of Lion's Bay. The tide was helping them now, and they picked up considerable speed as they gently pitched over small and regular waves, gliding ever out toward the open sea.

Sailors scrambled up the single mast to loosen the ropes holding the rolled-up square sail. Other sailors secured the lines on the gunwales, and the ship surged forward as the sail took its first deep breath. Once the oarsmen had been relieved, the Marie-Pierre was in full sail, and for the first .time, Captain Isnardon left the bridge for a leisurely stroll on the deck.

He avoided the merchants as their profession seldom had much of interest to share with a man of the sea. The Franciscans, on the other hand, were more than happy to share their communal store of Provençal wine with their host. The oldest of the friars even recounted the story of having met St. Francis himself on one of their journeys. They had found him quite an affable fellow, and not averse to sharing a hearty laugh, either. They also spoke of Paris and the conflict growing between the university students and officials on the one hand and the locals, led by the archbishop, on the other. "The students went on strike, and rioting broke out all over the left bank. Finally, the pope himself was forced to intervene in order to make peace. He placed the university under his personal patronage so that the locals, even the archbishop, couldn't touch them."

"I'll wager that didn't go over well with His Grace in Paris," commented the captain.

"Indeed not, but the students loved it, and they called off the strike and returned to classes. You might say the stratagem worked. The masters could go on lecturing on anything they wanted without fear of the local authorities. I guess everybody was happy, except for the archbishop."

The captain gave a philosophical shrug. "Well, you can't please everybody, can you?"

The skipper and the friars exchanged a good chuckle.

As the sun continued to climb in the sky, they spotted a larger silhouette looming to their left, an assemblage of blocks with which children are wont to play. Captain Isnardon could discern the vanishing forms of galleons, much larger than they looked from that distance, following the tide into the massive port of Marseilles. So, this was the ancient Mediterranean commercial center the Romans had called Marsalla, through which the riches of the eastern Roman world passed to Western Europe, beyond Italy. Departing ships would be waiting for the reversal of tides before venturing out, but one could only imagine what a huge number of them maintained the corridors of trade between Provence and points north on the one hand and Italy, North Africa, and the Byzantine east on the other. Not that these waters, teaming with commerce, were as safe as they had been under Roman hegemony.

Isnardon had told the friars that they would pass on the Italian side of the islands of Corsica and Sardinia, staying as far from those contested islands as the narrow passage between them and the Italian Peninsula permitted. The other alternative would take them out of their way, toward the Balearic Islands, back around Sicily to the east, down almost to Arabic North Africa, and back up the west coast of Italy. Such a journey would be entirely too long and too dangerous. Instead, they would risk the eastern coast of Sardinia, despite the ongoing war between the city-state of Genoa and the Republic of Pisa for control of Sardinian shipping. Bands of Pisan "privateers" sailed these waters to intercept and loot the ships bringing supplies to Genoa. If their Terracina-bound vessel were mistaken for one bound for Genoa, they risked being stopped, boarded, and searched, or much worse. These days, there was simply no way to maintain the Mediterranean trade without risk.

Meanwhile, even on the relatively calm waters of the gulf, Christobol was still hanging over the side of the ship, looking like the ghost of a valiant knight.

When the friars paid the company an amiable visit, Teresa asked one of the brothers, who introduced himself as Padre Tomaso, if he had any ginger, mint, or lemon, with which she could treat her patient. The friar obliged with a supply of ginger and one lemon, for which Mme. Balterra thanked him profusely.

She pried Sir Christobol from the gunwale and encouraged him to take her simple remedies. Little by little, according to Teresa, his facial pallor began to acquire a rosier hue. Without any preamble, she went over to the port side to share her treatment with one of the merchants who appeared to be in a similar condition. She quickly assumed the role of the ship's doctor and was afforded the respect and freedom of movement that such an office entailed.

CHAPTER 26

The shipping traffic into Marseilles had just thinned out when a large number of vessels crept up the eastern horizon on their trajectory towards Nizza, then a Milanese port. The coastline was not at all visible, but the mountains almost directly behind them loomed jagged and white like the shoulders of a sleeping giant. The sun was high and strong. The sky admitted not a single cloud, and the water had turned the most amazing light blue that Aidor almost wanted to reach out of the boat and drink it.

Paire Miquel must have nodded off, because, when he bolted awake, he had no idea where he was. The position of the sun, starting its westward and downward path, told him that it was midafternoon. He was pleased to observe that Aidor was amusing himself, admiring the sword of one of the merchants. Christobol, who had quite recovered from his seasickness, was chatting affably with the friars who had provided Teresa with her medicinal herbs and him with wine to assuage his thirst.

For her part, Teresa was treating one of the younger crew for rope burns he had incurred while unfurling the single square sail at the start of their voyage. Miquel noted that she had a certain ease and grace with which she engaged the seaman in conversation to distract him from the stinging effect of the ointment she was applying to his hand. He admired her competence and skill with people, which was no small part of the effectiveness of her treatment. Nevertheless, he could not help but envy the young man, whose hand was being gently caressed by his solicitous attendant, and for an instant only, he imagined that she might one day caress his hand in that manner. He willed the thought away as soon as it invaded his consciousness, and he turned his attention to the growing swells on the expanse of sea beneath them.

They were now well beyond the gulf and rounding of the tip of Corsica, moving into the Ligurian Sea. The wind had picked up some in this narrow passage between the rocky island and the Italian mainland, but the ship proved herself remarkably stable, maintaining a steady course and direction. Genoa could not have been far to their left, but despite the fact that this was the principal corridor between Genoa and the islands of Corsica and Sardinia, there were no ships visible on the horizon, either coming or going. Captain Isnardon, who was once again walking the deck, looked worried.

"The absence of shipping can mean only one thing," he confided to the scholar-priest. "There has been naval action in these waters recently, and regular shipping is staying clear. Hopefully, we're too small to be perceived as a threat to anyone and will be allowed to slip by without incident."

"How much weaponry have we on board, Captain?" asked the priest.

"A few swords and daggers, I imagine, for close combat, but nothing in the way of archery except for one crossbow, which we keep below decks."

"I would get it out and ready, Captain, if I were you."

"I've already sent for it. Our biggest worry is our own men. They're merchant seamen, not soldiers. What they'll do under attack is anyone's guess."

"I have a feeling we'll find out soon enough," remarked Miquel, feeling for his own sword and scabbard in the folds of his robe. "A quick prayer wouldn't do us any harm, either."

"By all means," said the grim-faced captain.

Paire Miquel interrupted Teresa's caretaking long enough to suggest that she take herself and Aidor below deck.

"I have not come this far not to be willing or able to protect myself and my child," she said, sounding a distinct note of defiance.

Paire Miquel was about to argue the point when he realized that after her ordeal with the Inquisition, she had evidently come a long way toward recovery in body and in spirit. She was, he admitted, the bravest person he had yet encountered in his travels. Finally, he relented and told her to secure a sword and dagger from Captain Isnardon. The ship was placed on combat alert, and the silent waiting had its effect on both conversation and morale.

Finally, a seaman atop the sail rigging spotted a formation of vessels approaching. Captain Isnardon stared to the southeast, where four large dots on the horizon gradually attained the outline and size of galleys heading towards them at high speed. The captain knew that galleys were normally used as warships rather than merchant vessels because they were fast and displayed great maneuverability. It was clear, even at this distance, that their intention was to overtake them. They were long and sleek, propelled by slim, multiple sails and no fewer than twenty-six oars each on the port and starboard sides. They had chosen their approach well, since they had caught their prey in a narrow strait between Corsica and the Italian Peninsula, effectively blocking escape to the south. The ship's only hope lay in outrunning them to the southwest and making it to the strait between Corsica and Sardinia, where the water was too shallow for the galleys to pass. The oars were quickly manned, and the ship tacked to the wind on a southwest heading.

The same wind and currents that were helping the ship also worked for the approaching galleys, who had gained so much on their prey that the colors and crest of Pisa were clearly visible. Christobol speculated that they were Pisan privateers policing these waters to enforce a blockade of supplies between Genoa and points south. Miquel wished that they could have explained to their pursuers that their port of origin was further north.

Anyone who could be spared from navigating, including Miquel, Christobol, the friars, and the merchants, manned the sides of the deck with swords and knives. Teresa convinced the captain that she had sufficient upper-body strength to man the crossbow, which was positioned in the bow, next to a tar fire. She was poised to hurl flaming projectiles at approaching galleys as soon as she was told they were within range.

Still, their pursuers were closing, and the distance to the narrow straits was a good quarter of an hour away. "Will they ram us and sink us, or will they board us, take our cargo, and sink us?" asked Christobol.

On the bow, Teresa had prepared her arrows, wrapped tightly in rags and soaked with tar. Artor, to her right, who had come from below to help his mother, held a torch aloft, ready to light each arrow. They heard the captain's voice ring out, "Loose arrows," and the first flaming projectile took to the air in the direction of the approaching galley. The arrow fell short, into the sea, but the next one landed, and the next one, until the galley turned away, engulfed in flames.

So intently were they fixed on the menace to the south that they failed to notice the approach of another fleet to the east, which deftly threaded the needle between themselves and the approaching attackers.

Suddenly they turned their heads to see four galleys displaying the colors of Genoa firing volleys of flaming arrows and driving away or destroying the ships that had violated their waters to interdict the single merchant vessel from Aigues Morts.

CHAPTER 27

Putting as much distance between themselves and the battle as they could, the *Marie-Pierre* made for the strait of Sardinia. One of the Genoese ships followed them in and signaled an offer of assistance if needed. Captain Isnardon told the captain of the *Sant'Agata* that he was headed for Terracina and that he would appreciate an escort out of contested waters. The captain readily agreed, and he stayed onboard the *Marie-Pierre* long enough to partake of the Isnardon's private store of wine.

The Genoese guest advised Isnardon to give the port of Pisa as wide a berth to the west as he possibly could in case word of their encounter had reached there. Normally, he said, the Pisans didn't harass any shipping to the south for fear of raising the ire of either the pope or the emperor in Naples. The captain of the *Sant'Agata* then returned to the rest of the Genoese fleet to arrange for the escort.

Teresa was relieved that no harm had come to her son, and Christobol was already writing a poem about the sea battle, comparing it to the Greek victory over the Persians at Salamis. As for Paire Miquel, he was struck by the image of Teresa shooting flaming arrows at their attackers like Artemis leading the hunt. She was simply extraordinary, but then she had to be, in order to survive. In the afterglow of battle, he felt no shame about his admiration for this singularly strong woman. He wondered at her readiness and ability to fight, and then he recalled that she was a mother fighting for her child's life, and he pitied any man who stood in her way.

Nevertheless, through the night, Miquel and Christobol took turns standing guard between Teresa and the groups of drinking and amorous sailors. Situated as they were on the north end of Sardinia, just facing the southern end of Corsica, they felt at once safe for the night and anxious to get out of these troublesome waters. Only Theresa and Aidor were tired enough to get a good night's sleep.

Just after dawn, they downed a hasty meal of dry bread and wine, far advanced on its way to becoming vinegar, and set off, following the coast of Sardinia southward. The island was thickly forested and, in the center, jagged and mountainous. It was clearly not a very welcoming place, but the closer to it they dared to sail, the further they were from Pisa and the coastal areas that the Pisans controlled.

When they sighted landmarks approximately halfway down the coast of Sardinia, the captain of the *Sant'Agata* signaled them that the Genoese escort was turning back. They waved their thanks and sped on, ever closer to their destination and, they hoped, safety. A few hours later, they turned northeast and headed in the direction of Terracina, in Latium, just a three hours' journey from Rome.

The sea was choppy from a sudden increase in winds, but they saw no other ships until they were close enough to the Italian mainland to spot the outlines of houses and mountains in the background. They discovered they had an escort of dolphins, who acted as if they were expected, and the friendly waving of returning fishermen and merchants laden with goods. They had expected a sleepy little village, but Terracina was a lively port, its docks filled with stacked crates of cargo and people busily loading, unloading, and inventorying the contents.

The crew unfixed the sail, and the oarsmen carefully moved the *Marie-Pierre* to its moorings, steadily reducing speed as it drew nearer to the dock. As if they were expecting something, people began to gather as the crew threw their lines to waiting dockworkers and the ship finally was pulled to a stop. A space was cleared for the passengers and the unloading of the ship's cargo.

Christobol was leading the line of passengers down the gangplank when suddenly they were surrounded by strangers, who mostly looked ragged and hungry, their hands outstretched as they asked for a small coin or a spare crust of bread. The beggars grabbed at sleeves and skirts until Teresa began to fear that someone would make off with her son.

From out of nowhere, a gauntleted hand cleared a path for them and rushed them through the crush to a place relatively separated from the crowd. Then Miquel saw that the hand belonged to an armored knight.

He was soon surrounded by six others, also in armor, and the travelers were ordered to stand where they were. They noticed that their fellow passengers, the friars and the merchants, were not being likewise detained.

The knight proceeded to address them in an Italian dialect that none of them understood, gesturing with his arms to emphasize his point. Miquel, who had been to Rome and Bologna often enough to realize that this was neither Roman nor Bolognese, pieced together an understanding that their leader was the Signore Aurelio Frangipane and that he wanted the group of pilgrims and the padre, in particular, to come with him to face charges of heresy before the Holy Inquisition. The others, apparently, had to come as witnesses and/or accessories to his crimes. Miquel asked the knight by whom the charges were being brought, and he replied that they had received a message from inquisitors in France that the same Padre Michael had alluded capture and that he was to be detained as soon as he reached Italian shores to stand trial before the local inquisitors.

Christobol went for his sword, but Miquel stayed his hand, shaking his head as if to say that it was pointless to try to fight their way out of this. He was determined to prevent any injury or loss of life until he could think of another way to establish their innocence. Their fellow passengers, the merchants, had been met by their business contacts and were long gone. The friars, however, watched the travelers being taken away.

CHAPTER 28

The company was spirited away to a portion of the shoreline around the bend from the port, where three small boats awaited them. They rowed out to an old, dilapidated fortress built, they were told, by the Frangipani to defend the entrance to the harbor. More recently, it had been used primarily as a prison for those who dared oppose the seignorial rule of the Frangipane family. The prison had the advantages of being both remote and waterlocked, making the prospect of escape that much more difficult, so difficult, in fact, that the gaolers didn't bother to put them in chains.

Having been left to contemplate their fate until the Inquisition was ready to examine them, they passed the time socializing with their gaolers, trying to acquire the finer points of the local dialect. They noted the regularity of the changing of guards, and they concluded that they were, to all appearances, the only guests of the establishment, at the moment. The soldiers in whose charge they had been placed did not regard that assignment as a particular honor. Clearly, they would rather be home with their families or out with their girlfriends, and Miquel noted that the night guard was somewhat skeletal.

Cristobol paced back and forth, trying to think of a way to escape. "Even if we were able to overcome the guards, there's more than one gate we'd have to get through, isn't there?"

"And we'd still have to figure out how to get across the water undetected and without a boat," added Paire Miquel.

"Damn, this place smells like urine and rotting food," complained Christobol.

"Our best chance would be at night: fewer guards and harder to see us," suggested Teresa, looking at no one in particular.

"If only I could figure out a way to distract the night guards… Maybe I could fake being sick and you could overpower them when they come into the cell to investigate," Aidor said after a long, sullen silence.

"Those night guards would rather let you die than permit you to disturb their drinking or napping. They won't be the least bit curious about how much pain you're in," concluded Christobol.

"Napping," Miquel said thoughtfully. "We need them to nap a goodly long time, don't we?"

He didn't pursue the thought, because one of the gaolers came over to tell them that they had visitors. "Visitors," repeated the priest. "Nobody knows we're in here."

At that moment, they saw two solemn Franciscan friars following the guard to their enclosure. Beneath the cowls, the faces were those of their traveling companions from Aigues Mortes. One of them, whom Teresa remembered as Padre Tomaso, turned to one of the guards. "We've come to provide spiritual comfort to the imprisoned, as our Lord requires us to do," he said, looking obsequious and straight-faced.

"Make it quick," replied the goaler, seemingly annoyed at the interruption.

When the gaoler had returned to his station, the friar pulled aside both Miquel and Teresa, smiled like one enjoying his act of conspiracy, and said quickly in a low voice, "Madame, you apparently know how to administer medicines and herbal extracts."

"Yes, of course," she said.

"I have prepared a mixture of ground valerian root and white poppy in this little bottle." He pulled a tiny, cork-stopped beaker out of the sleeve of his robe. "Just mix some into their wine, and they will sleep like the dead for several hours, long enough for you to lift a set of their keys and make it through the intervening doors and gates. Do it tonight. Wait until it's very dark." He pointed with his thumb at the friar who had come with him. "My brother and I will be waiting on the seaward side of the island with two boats. There's a gate in the courtyard wall, that one of the guard's keys should fit. We'll bring you to safety before anyone knows you're missing."

"Thank you, Padre. You're the answer to our prayers," said Teresa, looking hopeful and confident at last.

"Now, behave as if nothing's different. Look despondent and without hope. This will prevent the guards from suspecting anything," added the friar.

"We will, Padre," said Miquel.

The friar took a step back, beckoned the group together, and, at the same time, raised his voice and his right hand. "Benedicat vos Omnipotens Deus: Pater et Filius et Spiritus Sanctus," the friar intoned with a glint in his eye. He then called for the guards to release them. One guard escorted them to the exit.

The group proceeded to look discouraged and listless, rarely speaking, even to each other. They agreed to do nothing unusual until the night guards had settled in. Miquel told each of them to avoid anything that might be taken as out of the ordinary, so they were careful even to maintain their usual complaining about the lack of privacy for Madame, the putrid condition of the food, and the absence of washing or bathing facilities until the guards told them to shut up and withdrew to their stations. Teresa even called back a guard to examine a rodent bite on Aidor's arm, to which he complied without either provoking an incident on the prisoners' part or effecting a remedy on his.

The sparsity of light in the dungeon made it difficult for them to estimate what time of day it was, until even the dim shadows dissolved into monotonous, cave-like darkness, relieved only by the newly lit torch at the guards' station. Even then, they waited until they were sure that the daytime guards had had sufficient time to leave the island by boat, arrive on the mainland, and go their separate ways.

CHAPTER 29

Finally, Teresa combed her hair as best as she could, straightened her rags to look less disheveled, pinched her cheeks, although her pallor could scarcely be discerned in this light, and called out, "Guard, would you care to share a goblet of wine with a lonely woman on this dark night?"

She hardly had to ask twice. Both night-shift guards competed for her attentions and pushed each other aside to determine which of them might sooner unlock the cell to release her. They escorted her, like gallants, to the small barrel that served as a table, pulled over another barrel for her chair, and invited her to sit down. When one of them went to pour a goblet of wine, Teresa jumped up and squealed that a rat had just brushed against her foot. The guards shifted their attention to the dimly lit floor, looking for the silent intruder.

In the several seconds afforded by that fruitless search, Teresa slipped a small amount of the sleep-inducing potion into the guards' half-filled goblets and stirred them with her finger. Trying to make light of the small disturbance, the two guards raised their goblets, toasted the lady's health, and downed their drinks.

Minutes passed. The guards continued to recount past accomplishments, each attempting to distinguish himself as the more valiant. Gradually their speech slowed, began to slur, and trailed off to silence. First one, then the other, willing for all the world not to succumb, let fall his moist chin upon his soiled jerkin and fell into a deep sleep from which even an enemy attack could not wake him.

Teresa pulled a key ring from one of the sleeping gaolers. She dashed to the prison door and, after what seemed like twenty tries, opened the lock and freed the others. Miquel cautioned everyone to be quiet as they wandered down dark corridors in search of an unguarded exit.

Christobol glimpsed a thin strand of light emanating from the hall to his right. He lurched in that direction, only to be restrained by Miquel's hand on his arm. Turning around, he saw his friend place a cautionary finger on his lips and urge them silently down the corridor in the direction of the growing light. Carefully peeking his head around the corner, Christobol saw Friar Tomaso sitting across from a guard who was slumped over his chair, blissfully unaware of anything going on around him. Padre Tomaso stood, placing his finger to his lips, and led the company through a narrow passage that led to the outer courtyard.

The place was deserted and deathly quiet, except for the crashing of the waves against the rocks on the other side of the prison wall. The group moved in single file toward the rusted gate that Tomaso had identified on his previous visit. Quickly Teresa fumbled with her ring of keys to identify the one that fit. After a few abortive tries, she creaked open the gate. To Christobol, the rusty movement sounded like a screech from the gaping throat of Hell, sure to wake everyone from miles around, but they managed to slip out unnoticed.

Friar Tomaso led them along a dark path, toward the sound of the pounding surf. Rounding a bend, they were able to make out in the gloom the outline of two boats and the stooping figure of another friar loosening the lines that secured the boats to two posts in the ground. Quickly they divided into the two boats—Christobol and Aidor with the second friar in one and Teresa, Miquel, and Padre Tomaso in the other—and pushed off into the darkness.

There was no moon that night, and the waves bounced the tiny craft like a plaything. The friars seemed to know where to go and how to keep clear of the landing dock regardless of the relentless currents. At last, they came ashore at a place as empty and dark as a hole in the night. Taking each other's hands, they waded to the stony beach and sat to rest.

Friar Tomaso again addressed the group. "Our destination is the Abbey of Fossanova, four hours' slow walk from here. It's the only place where the Frangipani can't touch you and we can all get some rest."

"But how will we find our way in the dark?" asked Christobol.

"Just stick to the main path north and east of here. It's the biggest thing out there, a Cistercian fortress in the wilderness. We advised them in advance that you were coming."

"Do you think that's safe?" asked Teresa, sounding alarmed at the prospect. "Do they know we're wanted by the Inquisition?"

"Oh, their concern is not with the Inquisition," replied Tomaso. "The monks don't care for the Frangipane family any more than we do. The Frangipani tax the common folk until they don't have a pot to piss in, while they live in luxury in their palaces, and anyone who dares to oppose them politically ends up in a barrel beneath the harbor. They're a bunch of thugs who consider themselves grandi seignori."

"So that's why you put yourselves in danger to help us," concluded Miquel, who had been debating in his mind the wisdom of trusting the friars.

"Believe me," Tomaso said with a smile, "anyone who is an enemy or victim of the Frangipani is a friend of ours."

Feeling better, the group struggled to their feet and proceeded along the narrow path, in the darkness. The forest hung about them like an ancient collection of bones. Aidor clung to his mother, but he felt her concern and began to sniff back tears as he walked. They dared not light a torch, lest they draw attention to themselves. Not that anyone was out to see them at that time of night, but they couldn't escape the feeling that they were being watched. Every branch that snapped under someone's foot sounded loud enough to give their presence away, and the owls and other nocturnal creatures gave evidence by their cries that the company was both seen and heard.

When the night seemed its darkest and most silent, three ragged youths leaped from behind a bramble bush on the side of the road and called for the travelers to halt. The youths held staffs high above their heads, and they seemed perfectly willing to use them, but Miquel noticed something else about them that held him back from using his own staff. The rags worn by their attackers scarcely concealed the skin and bones that lay beneath. Their emaciated faces were pulled tight, and their eyes, sunken pools emerging from hollowed-out sockets, looked desperate but not angry, determined but not happy. If Miquel was not mistaken, they actually seemed scared, although they had the advantage of surprise and they faced opponents armed with only their walking sticks. On second look, these attackers were scarcely more than boys.

Padre Tomaso, with that disarming smile of his, spoke first. "Do you boys want some bread? I brought a late snack with me."

"We want all your money," the lead boy said with a cracking voice.

Miquel lowered his stick. "I have some coins hidden in my sandals. You can have them. You needn't endanger this boy and his mother."

"We're really very new at this," the attacker said in a calmer voice. "We didn't mean nobody any harm. It's just that our parents are in debtor's prison, and we are so hungry. We don't have nothing, you understand."

"Your parents went into debt to pay their taxes to the Frangipani *and* put food on the table for your family, do you say?" asked Padre Tomaso.

The head boy nodded. He pointed to his companions and said, "They only came along 'cause I told 'em to."

"Then you're one of us," said Padre Tomaso, signaling to the others to form a circle and share what they had with the boys.

In a while, they were laughing, and the place didn't seem so scary anymore. They talked about how oppressive the taxes were but that the emperor didn't dare move against the signori because he sought to gain their support for his struggle against the pope. "It's more than my head can manage," said the lead boy, happy to know that *somebody* understood his problems.

"I have an idea," said Padre Tomaso. "Come with us to the Abbey of Fossanova and ask the prior if you can work on one of the farms on the property. I'm sure he'll pay you a decent wage so that you can get some food for your family. Only, don't tell Frangipane that you have a job." He winked at the boy, pleased with his own cleverness.

When they got up to continue their journey, the eastern sky was just glowing red with the emergence of first light. Pretty soon, the sun was low in the sky, and they saw in the distance the towers of Fossanova Abbey.

CHAPTER 30

The company ascended the hill to the abbey gates and were surprised to hear a degree of lively chatter that was usually absent from the premises of Cistercian monks. Miquel wrapped on the door with the full confidence of one who would not be accused of either awakening his host or interrupting the dignity of the divine office.

A postulate answered the door, after exchanging pleasantries with a group of workers nearby. There was still a pleasant smile on his face as he greeted Miquel and his companions. "Identify yourselves, my good fellows, on this fine morning."

"I am called Padre Michael, from Aquitaine, and these are my traveling companions. We're looking for shelter and rest from our long journey."

The brother gatekeeper noticed that Miquel spoke with a strong Roman-Italian accent. He also noticed that the three local hangers-on appeared more threadbare and less washed than their companions. He regarded them with suspicion, but nevertheless, he allowed them to pass. "Father Abbot is expecting you, Padre Michael. Please come this way, and I'll show you where you can refresh yourselves and rest."

They processed to the guest house, which the company was pleased to see had been cleaned and polished to be fit for the visit of royalty. There were two front entrances on opposite sides of what looked large enough to be a dining hall, but which actually turned out to be the monastery's second library. The separate entrances were for women's and men's dormitories, to guard against even the appearance of inappropriate conduct.

Miquel explained how they had happened upon the boys, and the doorkeeper quickly handed them off to another monk, who conducted them to the stables. The monk promised ample work to keep them occupied as well as reasonably well compensated. Next the gatekeeper indicated the door on the left for Teresa, while he conducted the rest of the group to the other entrance, promising them that the abbot would meet them at the chapter house after Matins.

A half an hour or so after the Matins bells, Miquel wandered downstairs and outside to wait for the others in the open air. Who should be coming back from Matins just then but Miquel's old patron and classmate Cardinal Ugolino di Conti. The Cardinal was dressed in the plain white habit of a Cistercian monk rather than the garb of a prince of the Church.

"Ugolino!" exclaimed Padre Miquel. "It's been years, decades, my good fellow. I almost didn't recognize you without your red hat and robes."

"It somehow goes against the concept of community to not at least try to blend in with my hosts in the recitation of the hours," explained the cardinal. "Anyway, I've been hearing news about you and the Inquisition. "Still trying to take one leap beyond, are you?"

"Actually, I've been doing my best to keep an innocent woman from being burned at the stake for witchcraft!"

"You'll get a sympathetic hearing from the Holy Father. He thinks all this witchcraft hysteria is nothing more than pagan superstition dressed in Christian robes."

Michael looked hopeful. "That's what I remember from our old teacher, but how do you propose that I get from here to Rome without falling into the hands of the Frangipani?"

"Oh, you didn't hear?" said the cardinal. "He's not in Rome. He's right here in Fossanova. That's why the monks have worked so hard to shine this place up."

"What a pleasant coincidence, to meet an old friend and an old teacher at the same time."

"It so happens we're here together. The pope's making a pilgrimage to ask for the intercession of St. Stephen on behalf of his brother, Luca's wife, Beatrice by name. In her day, I understand, she was quite a beauty, and all the family was very close to her. She's been ill lately, terrible stomach pains. I'm told that the pope's doctors don't seem to be able to do anything about it."

While di Conti was still speaking, Teresa emerged from her door and stood next to Miquel. "Permit me, Your Eminence, to introduce you to my associate la Mme. Teresa Balterra."

"Enchanted," said di Conti, extending the ring on his right hand to be kissed. Teresa looked at him rather awkwardly, after which the cardinal, himself a bit embarrassed, deftly moved his hand away to put an end to the incident.

"Ugolino, His Eminence, is a friend and patron of mine from university in Bologna," Paire Miquel quickly added to break the awkward silence. "That was ages ago, I'm afraid. If I'm not mistaken, he shares your enthusiasm for ancient herbal remedies, an enthusiasm he acquired from our former teacher."

"It is an honor to encounter a cardinal and a friend of my protector," the lady said with a courtly bow and a lowering of her disarmingly beautiful eyes.

"Which reminds me," added Miquel, to change the subject from his lady companion, "I have a manuscript of the translation of Aristotle's *Physics* from Fontevraud, as you requested."

'Thank you, Michael," responded di Conti, with a gracious bow. "I shall see to it that our treasure is delivered to the faculty of science at Bologne, as we discussed."

Before Miquel could reply, they were joined by both Christobol and Aidor, at which point they made their excuses and proceeded to the chapter house to meet their host. Di Conti promised to join them as soon as he had changed.

A passing monk pointed out the squat chapter house entrance on the far side of the church, and the travelers hurried in, not wishing to keep the abbot waiting.

CHAPTER 31

Chrostobol was the first to push open the ponderous, wooden door and catch sight of the elaborate throne chair in the center of the room, as well as its elderly occupant. Miquel, quick to follow his companion into the room, quite forgot himself and called out, "Master Savelli, or should I say, Your Holiness!"

"Well, well, well, Michael, my son, it's been years, has it not, since the old days in Bologna?"

"I'm surprised that Your Holiness remembers me," replied the scholar-priest.

"Remember you? You were my second brightest student. One of the highlights of my teaching career."

"Second brightest!" exclaimed Miquel, unable to restrain his vanity.

"My brightest student was a precocious child I tutored years ago who grew up to become the Holy Roman emperor. He's turned out to be a thorn in his former master's side, but he still displays the rare quality of knowing how to think, and I don't mind taking some responsibility for that."

"Frederick's reputation as a 'wonder of his age' is well known throughout Europe," said Miquel, having reined in his academic pride.

"Like yourself, he is very interested in recovering the work of the ancient Greek masters and the Arab and Jewish scholars whose work has been, until now, unavailable in the West. He's setting up a school of translators, similar to the Spanish one in which you participated, in his own capital of Palermo."

"It sounds like you actually admire the fellow," observed Miquel, a half-smile breaking on his lips.

"Just between you and me, I do," the pope said almost reluctantly. "His academic plans have distracted him from his pledge to go on a crusade for us, but I suppose he'd rather learn from the Saracens than kill them, and secretly, I can't say that I disagree with him."

"Nor I," said the scholar-priest.

The pope took note of Miquel's fellow travelers and turned to greet them. Remembering herself this time, Teresa curtseyed and kissed the ring on the Holy Father's extended hand. Both Sir Christobol and Aidor bowed. "And what brings your company to Italy, my dear fellow?" asked the pope, making casual conversation.

"I'm delivering a copied Aristotelian manuscript to my patron, Cardinal di Conti, and we are accompanying this lady physician of herbal remedies from France, Your Holiness." Miquel had determined to reveal as little of his situation and circumstances as he could manage.

"A physician," repeated the pope. "Perhaps the arrival of this physician is the answer to my prayers and the reason I am here, too."

Miquel's conversation with the Holy Father was interrupted by the approach of Abbot Francesco, a tall, straight-backed man who, despite being gray-haired, looked a good fifteen years younger than the pope.

"Excuse us, please, Holy Father," said the Abbot, to the relief of the rest of the company, who had allowed Miquel to dominate the conversation with the pope. Turning to them, Abbot Francesco expressed his apologies for not having greeted them sooner. "I have been occupied with my Roman guest, he said, eyeing the pope, who was in conversation with one of his accompanying prelates.

"Not at all, my lord," replied Christobol, anxious to get a word in edgewise. "We have been well looked after and have even had a chance to rest a bit after our ordeal."

"How did you manage to get away from the fortress of the Frangipani?" asked Francesco, in genuine admiration.

"Like Saints Peter and John, we had the help of some angels," said the scholar-priest.

"You'll find angels in short supply around here," said the abbot, "with the emperor on one side, the pope on the other, and, in between, the Frangipani filling the vacuum with their own brand of iron-fisted rule."

"Does Signore Frangipane take sides in this stand-off between the Empire and the papacy?" This time, it was Teresa who spoke.

"He has switched sides several times. For the present, he supports the pope because it's to his advantage to do so. However, that may be short-lived if the emperor pays his price for bringing troops north from Naples," replied the abbot, not trying to hide his dislike for the Frangipani.

"Are we safe here?" asked Aidor, still somewhat uncomfortable with all this pomp and circumstance.

"Frangipane wouldn't dare try anything with the pope in residence, said Francesco. "Anyway, even he cannot gain access to someone who has been granted asylum. That reminds me. Quickly, you must formally request sanctuary. It's part of the rules."

"Of course, we do," Christobol said on behalf of the four of them.

"Granted," replied the abbot, his manner and tone perfunctory.

A young monk, acting as porter, announced a new entrant to the chapter house. "His Eminence, Cardinal di Conti."

In swept Ugolino di Conti, his monk's habit replaced by an elaborate crimson garb, with a heavy, metal crucifix around his neck and a red hat on his balding head. He bowed to the pope and the abbot and then walked straight over to Miquel and the company. He pulled Miquel aside and, with a frown on his face, said to him in a low voice. "I sent my spies out into the town and countryside. The lord Aurelio Frangipane has surrounded the abbey with his men. He's furious that you were able to slip through his hands, and he's determined to kill you as soon as you set foot outside of monastery grounds."

"Does the pope know about it?" asked Miquel. He reached into the folds of his robes and produced the promised manuscript, for his patron.

"His Holiness has been informed, and he has instructed the abbot to maintain your rights of sanctuary at all costs. He's hoping to resolve this without confrontation." He accepted the manuscript and added: "and thanks for this, on behalf of the faculty of science at Bologna."

"Surely, the pope will not want to anger Frangipane at a time like this?"

"Nor does he want to betray an old friend," di Conti concluded after some consideration.

Abbot Francesco called for order and announced a banquet in two days in honor of His Holiness, for which preparations would be made in that very hall. The festive spirit was evidently, infectious, and everyone, in whispered conversation, began to overflow into the monastery grounds.

As he turned to leave, Miquel felt a hand on his shoulder. He turned to see di Conti. "The Holy Father wants to see you and the lady physician up at the abbot's house right away."

Miquel hurried outside to catch up to Teresa.

CHAPTER 32

Teresa and Miquel strolled up the path toward the abbot's house, allowing enough time for the pope and his entourage to settle into the quarters that Abbot Francesco had graciously given his most important guest. While they walked, they discussed what might lie ahead.

"He's going to look for some face-saving offer to make to Frangipane," said Teresa, her eyes furrowed in a look of concern.

"I suppose, in the great scheme of things, you and I are quite expendable compared to the future of the Church and the Empire," said Miquel, not even trying to sound reassuring. "Still, if he wanted to turn us over, I would think that he would do so publicly, in the chapter house, rather than call us here for the sentence, to make it a grand gesture, after all."

"He doesn't strike me as a man who bargains with people's lives if he can help it," said Teresa, her face again wrinkled in a calculating scowl.

"But can he help it? Does he have a choice?"

From the abbot's door, they were ushered into a plain alcove with a door, presumably to the pope's private rooms, on the far end. Pope Honorius himself emerged from the doorway and greeted both of his visitors. "How kind of you to visit an old man so promptly." Without further preamble, he turned to Teresa. "My daughter, would you repeat you name for me?"

"Teresa Balterra, Your Holiness."

"May I call you Teresa?" He smiled to help put her at ease. "I have a special favor to ask of you. My sister-in-law, Beatrice, has fallen seriously ill. I have called in the best physicians and surgeons in Rome, but they have been able to do nothing for her. All those charlatans know how to do is to bleed their patients or cover them with leeches, leaving them worse than they were before."

"I practice herbal medicine, Your Holiness." Teresa wanted to reassure the old man, but she didn't quite know what else to say.

"That's excellent, my dear. That's excellent. I myself have read a text by the Greek physician Hippocrates recommending herbal treatments for a variety of illnesses. I was hoping, praying for just such an intervention when I took Beatrice here on pilgrimage to Fossanova to seek a cure. It seems that God has provided me with you."

Both Teresa and Miquel looked totally unprepared for this turn in the conversation. Teresa could only stammer, "I make no such pretensions, Your Holiness."

"Beatrice is resting in the other room. Would you do me the favor of looking in on her and recommending a course of treatment?"

"Of course, your Holiness," answered the lady physician.

"I will show you in and then return for a talk with Padre Michael while you examine her."

The pope and the lady went in immediately while Paire Miquel took a seat and tried to organize his thoughts about these developments.

The pope soon returned and sat on the bench next to his former student. "Michael, my son, how do we find ourselves in a place like this?"

"It's a long story, Your Holiness," said Miquel, suddenly worn out with his travels.

The pope waved his hand in dismissal. "Please don't call me that. We've known each other for a long time. My name is Cencio."

"I didn't know it was permitted to be so informal with the pope."

"Since when would that have made a difference to you?" Honorius broke into one of his broad smiles. "I never wanted to be pope, anyway. Ugolino and the others thought it was a good idea, or at least they thought that at my age, I'd make a good do-nothing, compromise candidate. I'll show them. I'll take away their princely privileges and make them work for the gospel for a change."

Miquel smiled but said nothing.

"You know, the reason that error creeps into our churches is not because people are seduced by evil. No, no. It's because they don't know Christ's teachings, and the reason they don't know is because we don't instruct them. Do you know how many illiterate priests we have? Why, two weeks ago, I removed a bishop who had forgotten how to read. He couldn't even read the Scriptures or properly say Mass. They think that just because they are the second or third sons of wealthy families that they are entitled to a posting to some diocese or monastery, when all they know how to do is break someone's head while sitting on a moving horse."

This was the kind of thing that Miquel remembered from his old teacher. "You should have stayed at the university and not let them take you to Rome."

"More and more, I think the universities are the solution to our problems. There, at least, people can be exposed to the theology of the fathers and study Scripture."

"But there are so many dioceses and parishes in remote places and only a few great universities." Miquel was enjoying the spirit of the dialogue, as in the old days.

"That's why I think that the pope—that I—should sponsor young theology students to go to the universities to gain the knowledge and then disperse it to all the dioceses of the world to spread that knowledge to all the bishops and priests they can get to. Education is the answer, my son."

"Seminary training and the mendicant friars, the Franciscans, the Dominicans, and the Carmelites, go around bringing the same message to the people," added Miquel.

"All the better," said the pope, looking animated and suddenly ten years younger.

The door to the back room opened, and Teresa came out, smiling. Both the Holy Father and Miquel stood expectantly. "I found Beatrice to be suffering from a profound pallor and a generalized weakness of the limbs. I sent a servant to the kitchens to ask the cooks to pound turmeric, sesame seeds, raisins, and dried dates into a powder and mix it with some red wine. She should take this mixture three times a day. I also recommended a strong regime of green vegetables, fresh air, and exercise. In a couple of days, she should be 'sano come un pesce.'"

The pope was delighted, and he assured both Miquel and Teresa that he was very much in their debt. Miquel brought up the unpleasant subject of Frangipane, but the pope dismissed the subject with a wave of his hand and promised to personally address the matter of this little man later.

CHAPTER 33

Two days later, after the singing of vespers, the gates of Fossanova Abbey were opened for the arrival of dignitaries from Naples, in the south, and as far north as Florence. Tables were erected in the spacious chapter house, with high-backed chairs and candelabra that the mayor of Terracina had ordered brought in for the occasion. The stores were packed with meats, fish, vegetables, cheeses, and sweets donated by all the nearby villages and farms, so much so that Abbott Francesco winced at the thought of all the waste and all the families, impoverished by taxation, that could have been fed with the superfluidity. This papal visit was, perhaps, more of an honor than the monastery was meant to bear.

Paire Miquel and the company were in a rather festive mood themselves after Teresa's successful treatment of the pope's sister-in-law. They could afford to be somewhat optimistic about their prospects here after such a long and hurried journey from place to place and their string of narrow escapes. They wondered, in passing, how long they would be permitted to stay here, where they were safe.

Aidor was playing with some of the children who had accompanied their parents to the feast. Although he appeared to sense no danger—for himself, his mother, or his friends—there was, nevertheless, in his eyes, a trace of fleeting furtiveness anytime a new face, however innocent, appeared in the courtyard. It must have been the result of a vague sense of peril, although he did not seem to know from whence it might come.

Christobol listened to the musicians and acquainted himself with new melodies and rhythms from familiar instruments, although he could not quite make out the lyrics of the singers. Notwithstanding all this distraction, he was also haunted by the plain chanting of the hours that he heard emanating from the abbatial church. The simple rising and falling of unaccompanied voices awakened in him memories of a more peaceful life, a time without danger or loss. He had left this life behind in his pursuit of his chivalric and poetic dream. Did this life still hold an allure for him? He didn't know for sure, but he did know that he had a duty to Miquel, Teresa, and Aidor that he could not discharge by staying in a place like this.

A procession commenced, amid polyphonic singing, starting with two straight rows of altar servers in cassocks and surpluses, each carrying a beeswax candle. They were followed by rows of choir monks, their hands tucked in their sleeves, local parochial clergy, and three visiting bishops in purple robes. Next came visiting cardinals in their scarlet robes and hats, and lastly, in walked the Holy Father, in red and white regalia, limping along with evident discomfort radiating from his aged legs and hips.

Just when Teresa thought that nothing could even vaguely spoil the festive spirit of this day, the gates opened even wider than before and filled with retainers and courtiers surrounding the equestrian figure of il signore, Aurelio Frangipane, here to usurp the role of host to the pope and share in the adulation of the crowd. He cantered up to the Holy Father, his horse kicking dust on the pontiff's robes. From his mount, Frangipane bowed, and the pope bowed in return, looking, for all the world like a deferential subject. They proceeded together, the pope limping on foot and the lord on horseback, never thinking to offer the old man a seat. They exchanged a few words during the procession, but no one could make out what they said.

Upon entering the chapter house, pope and signore made their way to the central seats on the raised dais, and the Bastanès company was ushered to a humbler placement at the tables below. To everyone's surprise, the elderly Beatrice, sister-in-law of the pope, was also shown a seat on the dais. She looked tired but otherwise well, and Pope Honorius appeared very happy to see her.

The meal passed without incident, and afterward the dignitaries retired to the abbot's residence for some private discussions. The pope, the cardinals (including di Costi), and Signore Frangipane were there, as were the mayor of Terracina and his aldermen. Surprisingly enough, and at the pope's express request, Abbot Francesco escorted two other visitors, Teresa Balterra and Paire Miquel, both of whom felt so out of place that they slunk into a corner and tried to avoid eye contact with anyone.

They did not fail to escape the notice, however, of Frangipane, whose eyes glared in their direction with an intensity and malevolence that il signore didn't even try to disguise. He approached the papal throne, but Honorius held up his hand to indicate that he had an announcement to make.

Frangipane frowned and forced his way back to where Teresa and Miquel were standing. "You know, one day, the pope must go back to Rome, and one day you must leave this monastery. Step one foot outside, and you're mine."

Miquel just stood in place and waited for the pope to speak.

CHAPTER 34

Cardinal Ugolino di Costi approached the papal throne and whispered something unintelligible in the pontiff's ear. "We'll have to do something about that," replied the Holy Father. By degrees, the whispering in the room fell silent.

Pope Honorius flashed his most benevolent smile as, with difficulty, he rose to his feet and addressed the assembled dignitaries. "My friends, I cannot express to you my gratitude to God and to the offices of one of us, in particular, to have brought about the miraculous recovery of my sister-in-law, my dear brother Luca's sweet Beatrice. She and I made this pilgrimage to Fossanova to pray for aid and guidance, and both have been given to us in the person of Mme. Teresa Balterra, here present."

Applause immediately broke out throughout the room, with the exception of the aristocratic hands of Frangipane.

The pope continued: "Aside from publicly thanking her, I wish to take this occasion to announce that I have decided to appoint her official physician to the Vatican, effective immediately."

Again, there was generalized applause, but this time, Frangipane raised his pointing figure and interrupted the applause to speak. "I wish to inform Your Holiness that the Holy Inquisition has just narrowly avoided this woman's conviction for witchcraft and has not fully resolved many aspects of her character."

"I am happy to note that those of us assembled here have not, as yet, fully resolved many aspects of your character, my lord, a fact for which you should be very grateful."

The comment provoked a round of laughter.

Frangipane raised his voice a bit louder, perhaps louder than he intended. "But the Inquisition reports that her mother was *Jewish*."

"So, if I remember correctly, was the mother of Jesus. Shall we consider another for the role of our Savior on the basis of that?"

Frangipane was just enough off balance to forget himself when he should have realized that he had been outmaneuvered. "Holy Father, may I remind you that these prisoners escaped my custody and thus avoided the call to justice."

"I'm afraid that the father abbot has granted them sanctuary in accord with the rule of his order and there is nothing that you or I can do about it."

"You're the pope, for God's sake. You know you have the authority to overrule him and hand them over."

"There's another thing," said the Holy Father. "I have decided this morning to form a delegation to travel to Palermo for the purpose of negotiating a peace with Emperor Frederick. Padre Michael lo Scozzese is part of that embassy."

Frangipane was beside himself. "What qualifications does he have as a diplomat?"

"He speaks seven languages, has been to more places than you can pronounce, and he has the qualification of having been appointed by me. Even you would not consider arresting an emissary of the Holy See, to whom I have granted my personal protection? Surely, you see that an attack on my representative is an attack on me?"

Frangipane was red-faced with fury,

"Furthermore, You will provide a military escort to assure the delegation is granted safe passage to the border with the Kingdom of Naples."

Il signore knew that the only reason that the emperor had not moved against him was because the pope had guaranteed the sovereignty of his family's heritage and that if he were to cast in his lot with the empire, the emperor would move in his own troops and absorb his territory into the Kingdom of Naples. "Of course, Your Holiness," he replied, unable, at the moment, to offer any other form of argument.

"I think that will be all for this evening. Thank you," said the pope. He raised his hand to bless the little group. "In nomine Patris, et Filii et Spiritui Sancti."

As everyone was filing out, the Holy Father stopped Teresa, Miquel, and Cardinal di Conti. "Please wait until we are alone. I have some matters to discuss with you."

CHAPTER 35

No one, except the pope and di Conti, knew what was going on. Miquel was the first to speak. "So, you want to give in to the emperor's demands, Your Holiness?"

"By no means. He and I both realize that the current, precarious balance of power is sufficient to keep the peace."

"Then, why are you sending a delegation?" asked the red-haired priest.

"So that you could leave here unharassed by the Frangipani, of course, and so that you may befriend and work for the Emperor."

Teresa finally spoke up. "Don't you want us to be brought before the Inquisition, Your Holiness?" She was at a loss to make sense of this.

"In the beginning, I thought it might be a good idea to establish rules of evidence to ensure that those accused of heresy might be assured a fair trial, but then people in power got the idea that they could use it as a kind of threat that they could apply against those they don't like or understand. All I ever wanted was a way to give instruction, encourage enlightenment, and afford people a way back. I never intended anyone to use it to punish people."

"And witchcraft?"

"Pah! Foolish, old pagan superstition, unfit for serious academic discussion."

Paire Miquel smiled, and Teresa raised her eyebrow in amusement. "I wish other ecclesiastici shared your point of view, Your Holiness," said the bewildered priest.

"Listen," said the pope. "This delegation will consist of you, Michael, Ugolino, and your bodyguard...What's his name?"

"Christobol, Your Holiness."

"And Christobol. You must tell the emperor when you meet him that you are thoroughly disgusted with my hesitation and procrastination. He'll like that since it agrees with his own estimation of me. You must tell him that I confided to you that I have no intention of threatening him with excommunication and that I am prepared to grant a two-year, no, three-year extension of the fulfillment of his promise to go on crusade. Tell him, furthermore, that I am prepared to crown his son, Conrad, as king of Rome."

"But that's a total capitulation to his interests, Your Holiness!" said Miquel, completely confused about why he was being given this message.

"Yes, yes, and Ugolino over there will be furious and will denounce you as a rank amateur and a traitor and that things said to a dear former student are not meant to be divulged to our adversaries as if they were policy. This will convince the emperor that what you said is the truth, and he will stop massing forces against his northern frontier to defend himself."

"Then you can withdraw forces from your southern border," said the priest, finally catching on.

"Exactly. He can use funds from defense to further the school of Greek and Arabic translation at his court in Palermo, and I can divert my funds to sponsor university students to teach theology. So, everybody wins."

"You will forgive me, Your Holiness, but some may consider your tactics a bit devious," Miquel said with a note of admiration in his voice.

"And I would tend to agree with those who did," di Conti chimed in with a knowing grin.

"You'll get your turn, Ugolino, you'll get your turn," said the pope, evidently enjoying himself. "Michael, don't miss this opportunity to profit from the joining of two of the greatest minds in Europe. You two could really make such glorious strides together."

"You'll always be a teacher at heart, Your Holiness," said Miquel, feeling like a young student again.

Pulling Miquel aside, the pope said, "I have one piece of bad news for you. Young Teresa and her son must come to Rome with me. At my age, I can't spare a good doctor, even for the emperor...and besides, you have your priesthood to think of. You're an educated priest and an intelligent one. We need you.

"Remember, Michael, you promised to be celibate, but you did not promise to never love. You know that God IS love. You must cling to that so as to never forget that we are all lovable in God's eyes...but keep your distance, eh?"

"You're right, Holy Father. Teresa and I will not forget."

With no time to calculate what would last them a lifetime, Teresa and Miquel stole away to a large, wooded area, at the rear of the monastic enclosure, a place which the monks only visited when they were in need of a supply of lumber. Here, they found a disused shed strewn with saws, ropes, and axes, as well as an array of rags and blankets, presumably to protect monks' hands from slipping ropes. Hastily, they cast aside the tools, covering a portion of earthen floor. and put out one of the blankets.

Miquel fumbled with the strings of Teresa's dress with all of the ineptitude of an adolescent boy. Patiently, she helped him with this task while lifting his cassock around his waist, before he realized it was happening. Eagerly, they saught the bare skin, beneath the garments. Their fingers explored each other's flesh with lingering gentleness, each sensation taking their breaths away with the newness of it. They discovered and released feelings which both had suppressed for so long, that they experienced a release like the banks of a stream, in the midst of a driving rain storm. They enjoyed an intimacy so fine and so complementary, that each curve of their bodies seened to fit together like the parts of a single organism.

When he entered her, she uttered a sound like a bird being whipped by the wind in flight, and their movements were like successive urgent waves of an inexerable tide.

Eventually, their passion subsided into words. Those whispered phrases, the poetry of a moment, would continue to ring in their ears in the years before them.

• • •

The next morning, two coaches departed from the abbey gates, going in opposite directions. One was accompanied by a unit of the Swiss Guard, the pope and his elderly sister-in-law, going north to Rome. On horseback, Teresa and Aidor followed the carriage. The other coach contained Paire Miquel, Sir Christobol, and Cardinal di Conti, with his precious manuscript, and was headed south, toward the Kingdom of Naples.

PART TWO
THE LETTERS

Note

I concluded my notes on the story of Teresa and Miquel with a lingering sense of both doubt and curiosity concerning the two principle lives that I had considered in these pages. I realized that based on their ages at the time, years must have passed since their separation at Fossanova, about which I had abundant questions but no verifiable answers. Did they remain in contact over the years? Did they ever have occasion to meet again? Did they ever openly declare their love?

I was convinced that the record was silent on these subjects, but then, in 1991, during a research project in a newly opened section of the Vatican archives, a team of scholars uncovered a collection of letters, dating from the pontificate of Gregory IX (1227–1241). The find turned out to be a carefully preserved package of private correspondence between a certain Teresa (unidentified) and Miquel (also without attending biographical information). In tone and content, the letters were not unlike the more famous collection of correspondence between Héloise and Abelard in the twelfth century.

It wasn't until last year that these letters were translated into English and I was able to study them. I have reproduced a number of them here, as I am convinced that the reader, by means of these letters, will be able to piece together some details about these lives, so long obscured by the passage of time. Concerning this correspondence, the reader may draw his or her own conclusions

1

My Dear Teresa,

The route was lined with olive trees as we passed by countless farms and rolling hills of pastureland. The sun grows hotter as the day progresses, and I am grateful for the shade provided by the curtains on the carriage windows.

I keep imagining that you are with me, but every time I look across to the other seat, I see Ugolino, his sharp Roman nose profiled against the light of the window. How thirsty I am most of the time, not just for water, but for those unguarded moments of contact, the smiling and the luminosity of your eyes, so stubbornly determined not to succumb to the torments that others have leveled upon you.

Freedom was our companion on the road, although we had to be constantly watchful. We depended on each other in our newfound freedom, and we became very comfortable with that arrangement.

You know, all my life, I have been a believer in logic and painstaking, dispassionate research to arrive at simple mathematical truths. Even my love of God was more cerebral than emotional until He sent you into my life. You taught me that emotion is the companion of reason, not its enemy. You showed me that we are meant to think and struggle as human beings, with emotion, compassion, AND reason, not as machines, with simple, mechanical purpose. You helped me understand that empathy and love are stronger than duty and honor, but not necessarily contradictory.

This realization has made me, and continues to make me, a better man and a better Christian. I feel a closer bond with those around me who face the same struggles and the same choices. I feel more like them and less likely to judge them, without having taken the same path. This strengthens me for whatever trials lie ahead.

How is Aidor enduring the trip? You must ensure that he gets enough exercise when you make your planned stops along the way. Boys his age need plenty of exercise to ensure they grow up straight and strong, but don't let him wander too far away from your sight. The world is still full of dangers, and even the Holy Father cannot protect him at all hours.

The carriage is coming to a rest stop now, and we will have enough time to refresh the horses and ourselves. I will write again soon.

With All My Heart,
Miquel

2

My Dear Miquel,

The roads have become twisted and strewn with rocks as we bounce around corners and stop to remove fallen trees in our path. The riding was so arduous that the pope invited me into his carriage, with Beatrice and himself. You must forgive my handwriting, which reacts to every bump as if it means to invent a new letter.

I'm embarrassed, I really am. I'm not a young girl with a crush on her handsome teacher. I'm a woman who knows her own mind, who has a will and a spirit of her own, which she surrenders to no one except with her own permission. I have neither a husband nor a father to tell me what to do, how I should behave, or whom I should love. I am a mother, to whom my son turns for guidance in this changing world, and he really thinks I have answers for him! Perhaps I do, but are they correct? Do they reflect the truth of what I believe, or do they express the truth of what I feel and experience in my heart and in all my will?

It used to be so much easier to know what I should do. My role was set down since long before I was born, and it never occurred to me to question it. But then my father and mother taught me to read and to think and discuss and dispute. One thing I will always remember about my father is that no matter how strongly he disagreed with the opinion of another, he never raised his voice nor made the argument about the other person, his motives or qualities. Discussion was always about ideas, not people, and they could always share a glass of wine afterward, as if nothing had happened.

Men have the freedom to think their own thoughts, but women must look to a man for what is expected or accepted from her. As a little girl, I resolved to think my own thoughts, even if I had to keep them to myself, but even that caution proved insufficient to protect me from calumnious persecution of fearful men AND WOMEN who found themselves in need of answers.

Fear is the enemy, fear of the unfamiliar or the uncertain. But the human mind only stretches beyond itself when it faces uncertainty or unexplored wonders. God must have intended us to be secure enough of His love to use the intelligence He gave us to search and expand our horizons. Those, like you, who do so should be rewarded, not punished. But this is not what history has taught us.

Forgive me, Miquel. I ramble on without telling you how much freedom you have always assumed for me, as if it were something self-evident. I should not have survived this ordeal without you, and if I am being honest, I should not have wanted to. You have given my life new purpose and a joy in living that I thought to had left behind forever. God forgive me, I love you more with every day in which our memories of each other live on. Life and love are so intertwined that I shall not experience the one without the other. I pray that you feel the same.

Love,
Teresa

3

My Dearest Teresa,

My thoughts seldom stray from the joy I felt when last we held each other. Your strength sustains me as I look forward to our uncertain future. I tell myself we must go on this way, but I cannot bring myself to accept this separation.

My journey occupies all my attention. With my passage into imperial territory, my forebodings are filled with the prospect of what greeting their leaders may have prepared for unwelcomed guests.

Tell the pope that I reject his commission. Tell him I would rather go with you to some country cottage and harvest figs for you to make into jam to spread over homemade bread on an outdoor table. This is the face of temptation, the call of my inner self over the role I am supposed to play for Church and science at the same time.

No, I won't stop and go back. I'd probably never make it across Frangipani territory, anyway. That doesn't keep me from wanting to, but I also want to make a difference, reinvigorate our culture with ideas from other places and other peoples. I want to give the world a chance to make peace and actually learn something from one another. I want to make a new age possible, because that's what I believe God expects of us.

Some people think that the way to preserve our way of life is to seal it off from "foreign" influences and outlaw any ideas and progress that are not our own, like a city behind stone walls. But history shows that such cities die, not all at once, but by slow starvation and the choking off of commerce. War is only temporary, and its effects reversible, but contact and exchange between cultures are permanent.

The only important part of my life, that I cannot replace with a bauble from the East or the Islamic lands of Africa, is you, my dear. Your beauty, courage, and honesty are unique among thinking people I have encountered in my travels around the world.

Why do you put up with me? I find it so difficult to talk or write about my feelings, as if, by ignoring them, they might simply go away. But they don't go away. Instead, they build up and occupy such a position of importance within me that, I feel, one day,

I must burst and spill my feelings all over the page in front of me. My thoughts and feelings are out of balance, in stark contrast to the equanimity and clarity that your words give to me. I must learn to put my feelings toward some positive goal or purpose, or surely, I will go mad.

The other day, Ugolino and I met a group who had fled from Spain to seek refuge in the Kingdom of Sicily, under Emperor Frederick. Their leader was an elderly man, Rabbi Soliman Ben Naman, who said that he knew your parents and your grandfather. He is an enthusiastic scholar who has spent his life translating Greek and Arabic medical texts for Jewish and Christian scholars in Toledo. You would have loved questioning him on the efficacy of old herbal remedies. I confess, he has a tremendous sense of humor, and he talks of your mother as if she were as beautiful as you are. Based on your stories about your parents, I suspect he is right about that. He told me what his friends and relatives had to say about Palermo, and if only half of it is true, I can't wait to get there. It encourages me to think about a place where Christians, Jews, and Muslims can still live and work together, respecting each other and building on each community's storehouse of knowledge to make a better world for all of us. I mean, we all agree that there is only one God, although there are many of us. From what I've heard, that's what the emperor believes, as well. That's better for mankind in the long run than endless war.

There I go, drifting into these kinds of discussions instead of telling you how much I miss you and how much brighter the world is with you in it. I guess I'm just more comfortable in the world of ideas than I am in the world of feelings. For me, it's going to be a long struggle before I can make peace with myself long enough to be of any use to anyone else, especially to you.

Tell Aidor that you and he are in my thoughts and prayers every day and that I hope and pray to meet you both one day, in a world at peace.

With All My Love,
Miquel

4

My Dearest Miquel,

I am convinced that the self-doubts shared in your most recent letter, which you have allowed to torture you so, are detrimental to your state of mind and your scientific work. You cannot be at your best on the battlefield of ideas if you are constantly at odds with yourself. Everybody is made differently: more or less comfortable with some things and uncomfortable about others. Remember that I love you as you are, because of who you are. I don't want to change you, and I don't want you to change yourself because of me. Love and peace are about being different while we respect and love what is unique about the other. Having studied Islamic and Jewish culture for so long, do you not yet realize that? How else can we learn from Jewish and Muslim cultures if we don't, at least, try to understand and respect them? If those of us who practice herbal healing did not respect the cultures that have handed down their knowledge to us, there would be precious little knowledge to draw upon. Above all, as a Christian, I suspect that you cannot truly understand and forgive others until you have understood and forgiven yourself.

We arrived in Rome today. Frankly, I was disappointed. Like so many others, I had heard stories, since my childhood, of the glorious capital of the Roman Empire, a teeming city of one million people surrounded by palaces, temples, and aqueducts. What I saw were sleepy streets, old, ill-kept churches, and sheep, yes, SHEEP, grazing in what had, at one time, been gracious piazzas. Pigeon droppings littered the streets, and ragged children chased stray dogs away from piles of uncollected refuse. Rome has lost her former imperial luster, and Pope Honorius promised to demand a clean-up plan from the city administrators, one that will take many years and the commitment of future rulers to accomplish.

The quarters on Vatican Hill for Aidor and me are modest but clean and spacious. I have an herb garden in the back where I have begun cultivating parsley, mint, fennel, and mandrake. In time, I will build up my supply and add to my plants as I get them. If I need something, I have only to ask the Holy Father, and he is able to procure it from somewhere.

The other doctors in the pope's retinue have been openly hostile to me. This, as far as I can tell, is for only one reason: I am a woman in a man's profession. They say they oppose me because my remedies do not work, but actually, they fear me because they do. Like old women, they watch for signs of the pope's favor, and when he pays any attention to my work, they set about to gossip and spit out all kinds of calumnies against me. They have, I fear, abandoned all reason in this matter, and everyone, but they, notices this.

Because of this animosity, the other physicians have blinded themselves to the benefits of herbal remedies, calling them the superstitious ravings of old women who rely on the beliefs of the ancient pagan Greeks. They prefer bloodletting and leech application, which are as likely to kill a patient as to cure him. God help us if the future of medicine is in the hands of such men!

The pope has given Aidor a private tutor from Bologna who is one of the new Aristotelian scholars, having drawn his inspiration from some of the books that you and your colleagues have been translating. He is very much a new thinker, and he has fed Aidor's curiosity like a mother bird feeds her chick. Thanks to the Holy Father, Aidor now has access to the pope's private library, filled with rare books and ancient documents that no one else in the world has ever seen. Aidor has said that he will either become a physician, one who respects the wisdom of the ancients, or a knight, like his old friend Christobol. You must tell Christobol how much influence he has had on the boy.

Aidor speaks of you, Miquel, all the time. The other day, he told me that the reason he can talk to me now about his hopes and dreams is because of you. I will never find adequate words to thank you for that.

Know that I love you and that I live for the day when we shall see each other again, if only for an instant.

Love,
Teresa

5

My Dearest Teresa,

How could I have forced myself to turn my eyes away from you when I yet had you near to me? I feared myself, not you, as I know you have always displayed the wisdom of Athena in your relationships with mere mortal men such as myself. I should have trusted you more, shared with you my inner feelings, when we had the chance. Now that can never be. Please trust me when I say that I love you and shall love you until my final day on this imperfect earth. If God so wills, we shall be together hereafter, and no man will ever keep us apart.

I hope that your work in Rome is satisfying for you and that Aidor is progressing well in his studies. I told Christobol what Aidor said about becoming a knight, and he confided to me that I should tell you to advise against it. Here in Sicily, the knights sit around with no enemies left to fight. We Sicilians have good government, honest tax collectors, and a surfeit of painters, sculptors, poets, musicians, and architects. Recently, the emperor decided to patronize a new "school" of poets writing in the local Sicilian dialect. They draw from the traditions of the Langue d'Oc troubadours, and the peculiar mixture of Arabic, Byzantine, and Norman influences we have here to produce an entirely new kind of poetry in an entirely new language, one that may one day unite all of Italy. Christobol says there's nothing to do all day but listen to and write poetry. He's even brushing up on his Italian so he can be part of the new poetry. Here is an example of one he calls a "sonneto":

Christina, with arching brows and looks of ice,
Boasts beauty burned on smoothest breasts,
Enormous eyes that drown young lovers in a trice,
Absorbing guileless youths as birds bring food to nests.

Intoxicating force, my heart is helpless to turn away,
To sniff the wine and leave the goblet full, untasted.
The scent of thee, my longing, my desire is to stay,
Else turn myself to stone, my blood, my life thus wasted.

From thee, thy gaze of cold indifference drives me out,
And all my yearning, useless tumbles on thine ears.
My passion and my pleading, thou ne'er would think about.
The rains that rob the sun are nothing like my tears.

Thy cold disdain, my searing flame will surely overtake.
And in thine arms receive me; all doubts and fears forsake.

So searches our friend, in the secret web of language, to seek release from...he knows not what. Poor Christobol! Will he ever find his way?

I finally met the emperor this morning. I found him not at all remarkable in appearance: short, middle-aged, bald, and quite shortsighted. Regardless of whether or not he could actually see me clearly, he professed to know me by reputation (good or bad, I don't know). He said he had several of my Aristotelian translations from the Greek as well as some volumes of my original work among his collection. Ugolino and I didn't have to play out our little theater piece in front of Frederick (the emperor), since he appeared to take an instant liking to me and was very receptive to what I had to say. I told him that the pope wanted peace and that he was willing to concede to the emperor's demands.

Frederick kept squinting at me, but it wasn't due to suspicion or skepticism. I understand that the ancients used a glass bowl filled with water to magnify a page. I shall work on a lens that will accomplish the same benefit to aid the emperor in his work. This is sure to meet with his approval. It surprised me that Ugolino took an instant disliking towards the emperor. Perhaps it is Frederick's Germanic temperament that my friend finds so intolerable. Ugolino returned to Rome much sooner than I expected, and I have received no correspondence from him despite my having written to him several times. It occurred to me that perhaps he actually disapproved of the pope's concessions.

But I ramble too much about politics. I now realize that there are so many more important matters with which to concern ourselves. With light, my thoughts ever return to the image of your bright face, your knowing smile, your kindness in the midst of pain.

I would trade all the panoply of court and all that the emperor could offer me if I could hold you for only an instant—an instant I could make last for eternity!

With All My love,

Miquel

6

Dearest Miquel,

Forgive me for not having written in some time. By now, you will have heard that Pope Honorius has passed away. For all of his political dealings, he was a kindly old man, much as I remember my father, and I shall miss him.

Our lives have been in a turmoil since then, not knowing who will succeed him or whether his successor will dismiss my son and me from his protection and care.

I am constantly re-evaluating my position here and depending more and more on my private practice as an herbal healer. I have my own wealthy and influential patrons to sustain me. The countess from Umbria has come by carriage to see me once a month since becoming pregnant, an event which she attributes to one of my medications, but which I attribute to the increased attention of the count, since the counseling I gave the couple last year.

Although my work keeps me busy, and Aidor's continuing studies fill me with pride, my thoughts return constantly to you and all that we mean to each other. What if things had been different? What if you had not entered the courtroom during my trial and caught me in your arms when I had fallen into danger at the hands of strangers? I owe my very life to you. Without you, I would never have seen my son grow to become both wise and strong. I can only conclude that God sent you to me and that I must thank Him for this great favor. But my thankfulness returns always to you, without whom I would not be here to thank God. What can we do? How can we bear this life in exile?

With All My Love,
Teresa

7

My Dearest Teresa,

I, too, have missed the frequency of our letters, but life here in Palermo has been uprooted and turned to utter confusion by the events surrounding the pope's death and the delicate balance of power that hangs in the balance. The French king, the emperor, and the king of Aragon are all trying to influence the cardinals from their countries to elect someone more favorable to their interests. The conclave of electors begins in a week, and everyone is waiting and praying for a favorable result. It somewhat amuses me that so many people can pray to the same God for opposite things and feel themselves sufficiently justified before God as to expect them.

The first thing I did was petition the emperor to let me return to Rome (to you), as an agreement with the new pope (whoever he turns out to be) would be necessary.

Of course, the emperor sees things through a different lens. To his way of thinking, I am his property, now. He sees himself as sovereign in the temporal realm, a situation that the kings of France and Aragon find unacceptable, especially when it comes to their rival claims in Italy. The pope stands between them, the potential friend and foe of all. His Holiness must avoid being crushed by the forces on all sides that come to bear on the situation. The emperor wishes that the pope would simply get out of the way so that he could get to his enemies. That's why everybody has a stake in this election. I'm disappointed to say that he has refused my proposal as contrary to his designs. He intends to offer no terms to the pope, whoever manages to get elected. I guess he's optimistic that his candidate will secure the majority vote. Then, Frederick's candidate will already know the emperor's position and be grateful enough to support it, during his pontificate.

While everybody talks of politics, I'm finding fewer and fewer people interested in mathematics, optics, astrology, and physiognomy, unless they can be used to make better weapons or battle decisions. No one professes to want war, yet everyone seems to be preparing for it. They've slowed down the translation of Greek and Arabic texts, unless they refer to some long-forgotten military tactics.

If there is only so much wealth to invest and you have a choice between war implements and the furthering of science, it's evident which choice our temporal leaders have made. I'm told that Frederick is negotiating with Venice and Genoa for the sale of my optical equipment to see ships in the distance. I regret that my legacy to the world might consist of such a thing.

How much better is the legacy of healing, which you have bestowed on Rome and its environs. I can't help thinking that with the exception of you and a few in the healing professions, we have failed to make this world any better or safer than we found it. I used to think that knowledge was the key. If we knew more, we could do more for everyone. Now I have come to realize that in addition to knowledge, there must also be a willingness to set aside our own interest and desires to pursue, instead, the interests of others. The greater good is not just the village or the city or the county or the kingdom, but the world. Perhaps the day will come when men will realize this, but for now, there is only war, treachery, and deceit.

Where do people go to hide from this? Do you know? The saints founded monasteries where they could work and pray, away from all this madness, but we, with our ties to this world, with all of our good intentions, where do WE go? There must be another way to serve, to heal wounded humanity and end our dance with death!

Our friend Christobol has found a way of building himself another world, one for whom the rules are not written by kings and emperors, but by lovers, in whom he finds the same loving impulse with which God created this world and to which He wishes to restore it.

There has been a sickness in Sicily since last year, during which we have all begun to doubt our prospects. The country was seized by another kind of malady, not of body but of mind, born of fear and a feeling of helplessness. It spreads insidiously, like smoke or fog, over everything we do. Our appetites flag, our energy deserts us. The most stimulating and challenging of work bores us. We forget our friends, even our loves, so self-absorbed become our daily reflections and preoccupations. We flee inwardly into the protection of our own selves, and we postulate the worst from every choice of outcomes.

Will neighbors ever greet each other warmly again? Will laughter ever replace the prevailing cope of fear that covers Palermo like a heavy mist? Will shutters and doors ever open again, and will children ever again light up the streets with their play?

From my apartments, I have forgotten what the outside streets and walkways look like. I have begun to forget the voices of my neighbors and my colleagues. Days of the week have become so like one another that I often forget the day, the hour, the month, the year. I lose track of time's passage, or I experience the advance of time in agonizing slow motion, fearing that one day, it will stop altogether.

I feel so, so alone, without you or Aidor to make it worthwhile to raise my head from my pillow. Did I not believe that this would pass, eventually, I think I might have died from the malady of mind.

From you, dearest Teresa, I have learned this resilience of hope in a world that draws its strength from the despair of others. You have given me the courage to fail and try again. Without you, there is nothing that this world can offer that, in the end, makes any difference. Please don't take your heart from me.

Love Always,
Miquel

8

My Dear Miquel,

Today Aidor asked me if you would one day be my husband. I told him that it was not from lack of desire on either of our parts that this did not take place. I told him that destiny had written two separate volumes for us and that each of us must contribute our part to the book of life, without a backward glance or doubt.

I'm disappointed that the emperor has refused your request to return to Rome. At last, there seemed to be some hope for us. The cardinals have settled upon your friend Ugolino di Costi as the new pope. I heard that he sought the safety and security of the monastery of St. Gregory ad Septem Solia for his installation and was taking the name of Gregory IX.

I don't think he will be seeking any terms with the emperor, just now.

I was told I had to wait many weeks to speak with him about my situation, and that of Aidor, because he had many dignitaries and ambassadors to greet. Well, all of a sudden, he walked into my laboratory and asked me if I could spare him a minute. He told me that my position as papal physician was secure, as was the tutorial arrangement for Aidor, until he was old enough to attend the university of his choice (which the pope hoped would be Bologna). When that time comes, Pope Gregory said that he was prepared to sponsor Aidor's studies there.

The new pope also asked me to send his greetings to you. He said he didn't respond to your letters because he suspected that the emperor would be opening your official mail and he did not want to mislead you or divulge information to those who are looking for it. He assumed that my mail would be left confidential.

Miquel, ask the pope to recall you. The emperor cannot refuse him on such a matter as this. I have prayed for this day to come, and I know you have, too. Bring Christobol with you and tell him he can write his poetry here, in Rome.

My dear Miquel, I have read all your works and translations on medicine. Together we could begin the healing of this troubled world one patient at a time and leave a great legacy for future generations. We shall call it the marriage between traditional herbal medicine and modern science. You mark my words; a new world is coming.

I know, you see through my rationalization. I want you back for me. I want to see you, to touch you, to share my life with you. How can God judge me for this? Is there not a place for us, a place where we can shuffle off the burdens of our situations and be like children in innocent bliss?

I am no longer young, and you are older still. How much time do we have in this world to be other than miserable and lonely? I would trade the prospect of years of security for one hour of unfettered freedom with you.

I suppose the possibility of your coming back to Rome has made me shameless. I would never wish you harm, and I would never ask you to do something wrong for my sake, but my love sometimes prompts me to go beyond the norms of our stations. Please forgive me.

All My Love,
Teresa

9

My Dearest Teresa,

I have written Ugolino, asking him to recall me to Rome at once. So far, I have heard nothing, but then I remembered that he fears that my mail is being intercepted and he prefers to use you as his secret channel to me. Have you heard anything? The rumors are fast and furious that the relations between the emperor and this pope are deteriorating quickly and that they are bound to end with the excommunication of the emperor. This is bound to be met with reprisal on the emperor's part, and that does not bode well for Italy.

What does Ugolino expect? Does he think that the emperor will simply cave in, as his grandfather Barbarossa did? If he does, he is underestimating his opponent.

On the other hand, the emperor has not been reacting emotionally to all this diplomatic pressure. Quite the contrary, he gives me the impression of someone who is using as much pressure as he can provoke to serve as an excuse for his seizure of territory. He doesn't miss an opportunity to assert his territorial claims and support those who support the Empire. There's always something in it for him.

Here on Sicily, life is good, especially for us scholars. The emperor finds money to support our work and to provide us with books that have been in the keeping of the large Arab community in the south. He's even assembling a zoo for the study and classification of animals from the Arabic east and Africa. This is the only place, other than Toledo in the old days, where you can find Arabs, Jews, and Christians all living together under a supportive government, their best and brightest scholars sharing information, libraries, places of study, and the best of their cultures. If there were any place where your absence from me would be less intolerable, it is here, in a place where your grandfather would have lived in peace and plenty, as all of us wish to do.

Last year, the emperor finally went on crusade, against his better judgment. He did not try to take Jerusalem by force. Instead, he negotiated its surrender after guaranteeing the safety of all its citizens (Christian, Muslim, and Jewish) and by ceding to the caliph two Balkan territories belonged to the Christian Emperor in Constantinople! He, then, had himself crowned "King of Jerusalem," and hurried back to Europe to use his new title as leverage against other European rulers. You can't help admiring this man for his shear boldness!

For us, the situation has gone from bad to worse. The pope will excommunicate the emperor for the second time, and he will never agree to send you and Aidor to the realm of an excommunicated ruler. Our only chance lies in your ability to persuade him to recall me.

My hair is thinning, the red hairs turning white and mixing with the brown. I'm struggling to keep up my hope that I will ever see you again, and I am more easily tired than I used to be. Please stay strong for the two of us and pray for the day of our reunion. As I work to distract my mind, I feel my life shrinking away with the passage of every day. My misery is only relieved by the hope that we will see each other again and that our separation will not be forever. I pray for you every day. Please, please, don't forget me!

In Love and Agony of Heart,
Miquel

10

My Dearest Miquel,

I am so pained to read of your torment at our separation. I can only assure you, if there be any consolation in such words, that my agony is greater than I can find words to describe, every time I think of you, and you are not there. I dream of you and wake to find my bed lonely and cold. I, too, grow old, with streaks of gray amidst the black. I don't even know if there is a future for me, let alone what it will contain. I am physically wanting for nothing, but my soul grows cold and small inside of a heart that cannot be consoled. I pray that each day may be better for you, but I have no joy to send you from my heart with which to warm your own.

My work continues among the palaces of the wealthy and influential of Lazio and Umbria, but I miss caring for the simple ills and wishes of the people of Bastanès. I despair that life will never return to what it was, and I, too, feel lost in a world I scarcely understand.

I have tried and tried again to meet with His Holiness about your situation, but it seems that he is constantly on the road with one of his two obsessions these days.

The pope is a man of contradictions. On the one hand, he unceasingly visits archbishoprics and dioceses throughout Italy and Germany to censure or remove bishops who live in luxury, neglect their flocks, or even refuse to live in the diocese to which they were assigned. He has encouraged the institutional poverty of the Franciscans and railed against the selling of church offices and the preferential treatment of relatives in ecclesiastical appointments. On the other hand, he encourages the preaching of crusades to win back the Holy Land and halt the Muslim advance, and he promotes the status of the papacy as the de jure leader of the Christian world, at the expense of the emperor. In fact, our world has become less united and more dangerous. The future is less certain than it has ever been, and I am afraid.

I'm sorry, Miquel, if I have let my frustrations get the better of me. I am so worried that the world Aidor inherits will be a world less stable and safe than the world we have known, and where will WE be when my son needs us? I can't tolerate this uncertainty and anxiety. The world is spinning out of control, and we do not know what condition it will be in when it stops. I know that God's providence will protect us, but I wish you were here to tell me that everything will be all right. Please send me some comfort.

　　With All My Love,
　　Teresa

11

My Dear Teresa,

I was able to meet, alone, with His Holiness in Naples three days ago, and I've been searching for a gentle way to break the news to you ever since. Ugolino has refused to recall me to Rome. He said that he was very sorry, and since his facial expression at that instant was more like a disappointed friend than the pope, I believed him.

He insisted that I was the only courtier that he could trust. He added that circumstances necessitated that he should keep me close to the situation so that he might not miscalculate. based on what he thought the emperor might do. He said that I was to go back immediately to Palermo. Ugolino—I mean, Pope Gregory—noted that the emperor trusts me and holds me in his confidence.

If I were to return to Rome, it might disturb that relationship, and the papacy needs me to be close to Frederick. Furthermore, I'm the only diplomate with whom he has a backchannel, through you, to send and receive messages that will not be read by the emperor's spies. "Really, my friend, this is not forever. Be patient with me just a little longer, and I'll find a way to bring you back without risking everything." Those were his words, and that was the last time we spoke of my request.

I can't help believing that he is partially motivated by his zeal as a reform pope. He can't discipline the hierarchy and the clergy while, at the same time, turning a blind eye to his friend, who is also a cleric. I think he's tired, as I am, and simply wants this ancient feud, with the emperor, to come to an end.

A Roman merchant sold me a copy of a portrait of you that had been commissioned by one of your wealthy Roman matrons. It is my mortal sin, but I treasure it and keep it closeted in my room, where I may gaze at it when no one is looking. The painter has captured the depth and sadness of your eyes to such perfection that often I deceive myself into thinking that I search those very eyes myself. They are two crystal pools into which I only wish to throw myself and never emerge again. I trust that the Lord will say of *me what He said of Mary of Magdala: "You are forgiven much because you have loved much."*

I feel the burden of each day's dawning, and I long to be released from these heavy concerns and to rest in your arms for the rest of my days.

With All My Love, Always,

Miquel

12

Dearest Miquel,

Your last letter to me was so very short that I fear you have begun to lose interest in me. I know that your master and friend, the emperor, regales you with books and scribes and access to so many resources for your experiments and investigations. I imagine that you have no time to think of such a simple purveyor of herbal medicines as myself. The fate of the Christian world, I know, rests on your shoulders, depending, as it does, on the advice you give to both emperor and pope.

But I depend on you, too! Your portrait does not occupy a hidden place in my closet, but a place in my heart, which I wear openly for all to see. I no longer care who knows we love. City life is so open and sophisticated that it is not considered scandalous for clerics or married men to carry on alliances with young women of their own and higher stations. The pope's efforts at reform have not kept pace with the temptations that wealth from growing trade have placed in his path.

But I remain faithful to you, my love, as true as the herbs and roots that heal sickness and as true as kind words heal those who are sick at heart. This world is profligate, its promises perjured and broken as easily as one's image in a looking glass. Our love is built on truth, compassion, and a gentleness of soul that knows neither perjury nor deception. Our love does not ebb and flow with the fashions of the season. We must support one another through good times and bad, knowing that our true home is with each other, whatever the times portend.

I must tell you of Aidor, who, this year, will go to Bologna to attend the university. His ambition is to study medicine, to receive his doctorate, and to serve the rural population of southern France, among whom he intends to find our previous home. He prefers a peaceful life to that of the city, and he never forgets what true friends can mean to one another. I'm proud of him, and you should be, too. I thought that Christobol might have filled his head with crazy ideas of chivalry, but it was you who had the most lasting influence on him. He's an intelligent boy and conscientious about his studies. I think he'll make us proud.

Why did you not threaten Pope Gregory with telling the emperor everything about the pope's access to his secret plans, of your communication channel through me? Do you intend to dedicate the rest of your life to this kind of duplicity? Why can't you tell both pope and emperor to go to the devil and leave us alone? Haven't you given them both enough of your life? Is there to be nothing left for you and me?

I know, I know. I'm being very selfish, considering both your great work and the peace in Europe, which you play with like a toy, but do I not have a right to fight for myself, as all living creatures do? If not, why didn't you leave me to be executed by the angry mob at Lescar, where my life was not worth the rags on my back till you carried me away? To what end, my love, to what end?

I'm not angry with you, Miquel, nor am I angry with the pope or the emperor. It's been a long time since I have had to define my boundaries in accordance with the wishes and aspirations of a man, be he father or husband. Although I long for a man in my life, I do not surrender to him all that I may ever aspire to be. I believe, as you do, that God created woman to be man's companion, not his property. Why else would you have risked everything, including your life, to save a fragile widow, however valueless?

I don't know what answers we might discover in the future, but I pray for a future that might include a path to happiness for us.

With All My Love,
Teresa

13

My Dearest Miquel,

It has been many months now since I have heard from you. Are you well? Does your work exhaust you more than ever before? Where do your tasks take you these days: to Naples, to Germany, to Bagdad, to Egypt?

Oh, Miquel, have I angered you? Do you judge me harshly for the last words I wrote to you? I must speak from my heart, and I pray that your love for me will open your eyes to see it.

I am a woman, but God has given me a mind and spirit that cannot be contained, as if in a box. I made a life for myself and my son when no one else would openly acknowledge having us as their neighbors. I became accustomed to being a foreigner, an outsider, one to be feared and kept at arm's length lest anyone should become impure or contaminated. Lepers are treated this way all over the world, and you know, they even develop a sense of disgust for one another, so pervasive and self-loathing is their isolation. I have lost my ability to put customers at ease, to communicate a general sense of well-being with just a smile and a quiet conversation. People avoid me on the street, and customers take the medicine and run without a word.

I caught sight of my face in a glass the other day. It was ghastly, old, and terrifying. I can't remember the last time I laughed or even smiled into a mirror. This morning, I had the impression that my image had begun to disappear, to dissolve into the air. Soon there will be nothing there for anyone to see.

It's raining in torrents today. The streets are empty of shoppers and children. Rome is a lonely place, as if it were one visited by pestilence. The water strikes the roofs as if someone had emptied buckets of ice, crashing over our heads like falling rocks. The thunder cracks behind a covered market across the road, and the light pierces the window like the attack of something unholy. The rain fills the air in continuous sheets, and the streets are running with churning, bubbling streams feverishly seeking any place to continue going down to the swollen river. I am alone, sinking into oblivion, and no one comes to offer me an escape.

But I write only about my own feelings. Tell me, Miquel, that you are surviving all this and that your world is not closing around you, too. Tell me that the emperor has not sent you to Antioch or Alexandria for books. I don't know if the destinations themselves are more dangerous than the journeys you must take to get there. Every time I close my eyes, I imagine you in some foreign land, alone and friendless, and I ache to be there and to comfort you. I fear that you might find yourself in need of a physician or a chemist or just a companion to ease the loneliness of the journey.

Have you learned anything interesting, having studied the emperor's horoscope? Have I reason to be optimistic about the possibility of your return from Sicily? What about us? Have you read the messages of the stars to glimpse a view of what will happen to us? Why are you more skillful at helping others than you are helping yourself? Or do I misunderstand the workings of an astrologer or a seeker such as you are?

I find myself asking questions such as I've never asked before, about why we are here and what the future holds for us. Is this because I am evil, or is it that the mind cannot be content to remain in ignorance even about the things it cannot control? I read and think and pray that I might receive the wisdom to understand that which defies explanation. Is it hubris on my part, to want to solve the riddles of our existence, to penetrate the secrets of Destiny itself? Are we really in possession of free wills, or are we puppets of a Fate that is blind and indifferent to us?

These are terrible thoughts that haunt me like the ghost of my bygone life. I confess with shame that I have even envisioned taking my own life, but I cannot do it, not as long as it means taking my leave of you. In truth, the thought of you is the only thing that keeps me in possession of my life, else I would have died in Bastanès or Lescar, a witch and a cast-off from the world.

The agony of not hearing from you is taking its toll on my health. I grow old and thin, waiting for the ship that never comes and wondering if I will ever be deemed worthy to receive its contents. Please, please, come to me, my love.

From the depths of My Heart,
Teresa

14

My Dearest Teresa,

Do not harbor such thoughts of hopelessness and despair in your heart. My darling, as long as I live, I shall work night and day to return to you and put all this agonizing separation behind us so that we may finally have a life that is ours to enjoy and share with each other. I have been warned by those close to the emperor that if I try to leave his service, I will most assuredly be dead by the time I reach the Kingdom of Naples. Sicily is an island, and its ports are carefully watched. My face is too familiar to permit clandestine travel, and if fighting should break out between Guelfs and Ghibellines to secure my freedom, it would surely engulf all of Italy and much of Germany in civil war. My only chance is to secure a peace between these two stubborn adversaries and end this once and for all.

Such a state of constant alert, constant preparation for war, has begun to take its toll on me, both my physical and my mental well-being. I find that I can trust fewer and fewer people these days. In truth, I trust only you, my dear, to keep faith with me in these dark times. When I wonder what peace is for, and if it's worth striving for, I think of you, not the pope, not the emperor. After all, there will be other popes and other emperors, but there is always and eternally only one you, my love. How do we reshape the world so that our lives are protected rather than used? What overwhelming pride makes me see myself as the center of my world? What chaos would result from each person's seeking only his own happiness, no matter what the cost to others? Yet, if the happiness of all is not the goal of life, what value is there in living?

I have always believed that God intended us to be happy. Why else would He have made us desire it so? Has our life in this world become so twisted and distorted that, while we want happiness, we are condemned never to receive it?

You see, this is why I have not been able to bring myself to write to you, because my own thoughts have become so utterly depressing that I am loath to share my profound sadness with you and, in the process, make yours so much greater. But finally, you see,

I must tell you the truth. You are the only person in the world with whom I cannot dissemble, whom I cannot successfully deceive in any way. Oh, but I cannot be the agent of pain for you, either! I am so conflicted, because no matter what I say to you, I am either dishonest or hurtful. What am I to do?

You asked if I used my astrologer's skill to influence the emperor to do what I want him to do. I consider it a misuse of the art to use astrology to predict how people will or should act. To me, it is a complex mathematical puzzle whereby we can test the validity of prevailing theories about the movements of heavenly bodies. I have applied my formulas, for example, to the assertions of Ptolomy concerning these movements, and I have detected some unmistakable faults in his calculations. Perhaps we're looking at it the wrong way, but I can't arrive at an alternate hypothesis.

I know that I should be using my studies to influence events, but I consider that sort of trickery to be such a descent into dishonesty as to sicken my conscience as a scientist. I must do my work honestly and in pursuit of knowledge or not at all. Should I practice deceit of others and of myself, I shall surely lose myself in the process.

Tell me, my dear Teresa, of your work and your successes with your herbs and poultices. Surely, it must give you some comfort to see the good that you have done for many people. Have your enemies and detractors reversed their opposition to herbal healing, or do they continue to try to destroy your work? Be careful, my dear Teresa, not to underestimate the extent of their malice, if they see you as an impediment to their wealth. You must insist on only seeing patients within the grounds of the Papal Palace. Even then, your enemies can tarry until Ugolino passes away and take their chances with his successor to try to hold you to account. Please, please, Teresa, assure me that you will be careful. We must keep ourselves for our eventual reunion.

With All My Love,
Miquel

15

My Dearest Love, Teresa,

I have entrusted this letter to my friend Christobol for fear that someone might intercept it. I learned that my letters to you are now scrutinized, as is anything I do or anyone I meet. You will not recognize the hand because I have dictated these words to Christobol. I am bedridden and overcome by a terrible weakness. I fear my strength is leaving me and that my life force is, by degrees, ebbing away. Matters grow worse here by the day, and I have even tried hiding in an empty wine keg to get to you, but a loose stone fell on me, smashing the keg and striking my head. Now I have not the strength to try again.

I am now taken seriously ill, and I fear that by the time you receive this letter, I will have departed this life, which I so wished to share with you. The emperor has refused to release any information to Ugolino about my condition, nor has he agreed to pass any messages to me. He has become embittered and distrustful of almost everyone. I have sat alone with my experiments, star charts, and calculations, with nobody willing to pass the time with me since I have fallen from the emperor's favor.

I have placed your portrait, Teresa, on my wall since no rumor mongers pass this way, anyway, except for my confessor, who is bound by the secrecy of the confession to say nothing about it. I gaze at your face every day from my sickbed, and frankly, you are the only reason that I am still alive.

Someday medical scientists will understand the infirmity from which I suffer and devise a method to remedy it. In the meantime, I must languish in our general ignorance, a condition from which even the emperor cannot forever escape. I have passed long days remembering my sins and my achievements, but I have not lived so long that I would forget you, who reminds me always that discovering the truth is paramount and pleasing at the same time. Thoughtful people have always questioned and tested phenomena to better understand their causes and effects, but the more we study, the more we realize what we do not know. God intended it so, to make us humble, but not to satiate our curiosity.

But I digress. My illness should not be a burden to you, any more than my age should take a day away from your youth. There, you see? Even a sick, old man can appreciate beauty and health. I do hope you are well and that Ugolino has remembered his promises to you, made so many years ago. Please don't think of me except as a pleasant memory from our (YOUR) youth. I am a most insignificant man, not of any lasting value to anyone, even to Ugolino. My life's work is just the beginning, just the beginning. On the contrary, the people you have helped, both in mind and body, will stay well, and their children's children will also have children. So, life, thus nourished, goes on, and the good that you have done will never go away.

You are my good angel, you know. Before I met you, I thought that I possessed the key to knowledge more than any other mortal before me. After meeting you, I learned that as long as we do not know and accept what we feel, our knowledge is incomplete, our capacity to understand one another limited. Humans are living beings, body and mind inexplicably intertwined until we die.

I wonder if animals anticipate and worry about their death as much as we do? The animals I've seen after the hunt has brought them down are usually quiet and serene, as if nothing could be more natural than dying. Is that how I'll feel? Having had the privilege of knowing you, I think that I shall count myself the luckiest man in creation, ready for the adventure to come, hoping to share that adventure one day with you.

You must not be in a hurry to join me. You have many patients to heal, and you must see Aidor become a full-fledged physician, one who will assimilate the knowledge of the ancients with the newfound knowledge of present and future days to really make a difference for everyone. Think of being able to share that when we meet again and to appreciate our part in making it happen. I couldn't be prouder of Aidor if he were my own son. That's a little bit of immortality of which my choices have robbed me. Still, I know that actual immortality comes from somewhere else and that we cannot relive our lives through our children.

We must all make our own mistakes, it seems. Nevertheless, it reassures us to think that future generations will not make the same mistakes and misjudgments as we did. Perhaps they'll make their own mistakes, but hopefully, they will learn from them and pass those lessons down.

One of the mistakes I have made, at least before I met you, was to listen consistently to my head and not my heart. I have always had an inquiring mind that needed to make sense of things, to understand cause and effect, movement and mover, all subject *to immutable laws. Everything had to make sense, except for you, and you are more real and important to me than any amount of logic, proof, and discovery. From you, I learned that some things are worth risking your life for.*

I would gladly have given my life on several occasions to assure myself of your safety. I love you now more than ever, more than life itself, more than all our tears could ever wash away, more than I have ever had the skill, courage, or honesty to tell you before. I cling to the memory of you as if memory were still more real than present burdens, and I offer you my hand, over miles, over infinities of time, which proves more real than time itself, closer than any distance can ever be. I don't have to give you up; I won't give you up, as I slide so imperceptibly into eternity.

I offer my pain in exchange for the lifting of your suffering. May, from the moment that you receive this letter, a lightness come over you, as if you could fly to heaven and return to earth any time of your choosing. May you inhabit both this world and the world of our eternity, as a citizen of the Blessed City and the humble earth at the same time.

I wish you memories for a long life, as memories are both timeless and free from the constraints of distance. Just close your eyes, and you will see me standing before you and building a universe around your face. You are the star that guides my ship at night, and you are the majestic sun, which gives us life and warmth by day.

You are my compass, holding me to a steady course, such that through all my trials and false starts, I have never lost sight of you, my true north. I may not always say what I feel in my heart, but my heart never lets me forget that it beats for you. When the beating of my heart has stopped, the sound will resonate through eternity as the endless rhythm of our love.

My dearest Teresa, I have also entrusted to Christobol a box containing all that I have earned from Emperor Frederick, for the study of astrology, alchemy, physiognomy, the mathematics of artillery flight and optics, and various other studies that I have conducted, including translations, from Greek and Arabic, of the works of Aristotle, Avicenna, Averroes, and others. I have also included the stipends and living expenses that I received from both Pope Honorius III and my friend Ugolino, inasmuch as I have been able to economize over the years by residing in monasteries and other religious houses instead of purchasing my own accommodations. All in all, I hope that the accumulated resources may serve both you and Aidor, whom I hold in my heart as if he were my own son, for many years to come and in whatever place is most comfortable for you.

It is my fervent hope that you should never be in want for any physical comfort as long as you live, and that Aidor be given every opportunity to become as skilled a physician as God has given us in the person of his mother and my only true love. If this future is what my work has been able to obtain, then I am prepared to go in peace, having accomplished that which is most important to me.

My work of scientific inquiry is, and must always be, incomplete, but I die knowing that others are willing and prepared to carry on this work. I have read of a young Franciscan, in England of all places, by the name of Roger Bacon, who has conducted such encouraging work based on the empirical value of experimentation and the value of being able to replicate an experiment and obtain the same result. This is exciting work, which bodes well for the future.

I have not the skill at words to say goodbye, but as surely as my soul will survive my death and my soul and body will, one day, be reunited, so, too, am I sure that my love for you is stronger than death and will survive in our souls, forever.

I love you and will love you always,

Miquel

EPILOGUE

The rest, of course, is speculation. I prefer to believe that Teresa Balterra stayed in Rome after learning of Miquel's death and busied herself with her growing practice and reputation. Besides, she would have wanted to maintain frequent contact with her son, Aidor, to follow his studies and subsequent career. Aidor, I suppose, became a physician of great reputation, famous for his use of dietary alterations and medicinal herbs, in addition to the traditional medical treatments of the age.

No one knows for sure what eventually became of either Teresa or her son. Subsequent disruptions, wars, and invasions obliterated many records of the time, and with the seventy-year displacement of the papal court to Avignon, in France, little remains of the daily lives of Rome's citizens left behind.

With any luck, Christobol relocated to Florence, where he became associated with a group of poets who were giving form to a Tuscan dialect of the Italian language that, throughout Italy, was gradually overtaking the Sicilian as the fashionable language. It was rumored that he eloped with a local girl of the Pazzi family and was forced to flee the city with his wife, and set up a new life in Ancona, on the Adriatic.

The portrait of Teresa, the copy of which Michael refers to in his letters, has never been recovered.

AFTERWORD

The actual date and place of Michael Scot's death and burial remain a mystery. Part of the problem is that there was another Michael Scot (or Scott) who lived about a hundred years later and who was also known as someone who dabbled in what people supposed was dark magic. Stories about what we presume were two different men frequently get confused, and the more often tales are retold, the more fanciful they become.

Notwithstanding the myths and legends that have grown around that name, all having to do with our fascination for magic, one aspect of Michael Scot's historical contribution cannot be doubted. He was one of the foremost intellects of that age, so misunderstood by so many who have followed. His translations from the Arabic and Greek, as well as scholarly works of his own, contributed immeasurably to the explosion of knowledge fueled by the rediscovery of many works of antiquity, without which the European Renaissance, two hundred years later, could not have happened in the way that it did. Far from being silenced and punished for his groundbreaking work, he was sponsored and supported by two popes and Holy Roman Emperor Frederick II alike. He enjoyed a degree of academic freedom that was much greater than we have been taught to expect.

Michael Scot, however, was also a man. As is the case with so many famous or infamous persons, history has obliterated all trace of his essential humanity. It was my objective as a novelist to somehow get beneath the veneer of fame and myth and identify the very human person who took breath and found his way toward knowledge and truth in an age where both were valued more highly than we suspect. It is important that we see him in the context of his age, and not our own, and understand that education, disputation, and the pursuit of knowledge existed as the nurtured child of the age we so arrogantly call "dark."

This realization also helps us understand Teresa Balterra, a woman who was not the chattel of either husband or father, a woman who made her own life at a time when there were fewer possible ways in which a woman might be expected to do so.

Numerous examples may be pointed out in Medieval Europe of women who demonstrated a surprisingly high degree of learning, independence, and influence in an otherwise male-dominated society. Many of them, not surprisingly, came from the upper classes or the Church, mystics, abbesses, heiresses, and rulers of vast dominions, whose decisions and writings have greatly influenced European history and thought. Some of them are fairly well known, such as Emperess Matilda and Eleanor of Acquitaine, but others are nameless, whose husbands went off to war, leaving the management of their estates to the women: the accounts, the payment of taxes, the collection of rents, the hiring and firing of employees, the raising and leading of armies to counter invasions. If their husbands were fortunate enough to come back, the fact that they had lands at all was undoubtedly due to the skill, cunning, and ingenuity of the women they left behind.

In addition to the aristocracy, influential women were also among the products of the Church. Hildegard of Bingen, Bridget of Sweden, Clare of Assisi and Theresa of Avila distinguished themselves by their erudition and their writings. St. Catherine of Siena wrote extensively to Pope Gregory XI, calling him to task and urging him to return from Avignon to Rome. Many rose to become abbesses of great convents, administered lands, and contributed to the development of the literature of many countries.

I ask myself, however, what about the common woman, whose accomplishments lie hidden beneath a social history predominantly written by men? Did they win freedom of thought, and did they gain influence in their changing society?

There existed from antiquity the double roles of healer and midwife, the tools of whose trade consisted of a mixture of ancient herbal remedies and lore (largely passed on by word of mouth), talismans, tinctures, and incantations, which, while regarded by the Church as the survival of ancient pagan superstition, were largely tolerated and sought after because they gave people comfort and, for reasons unknown, worked most of the time. These professional healers were, in large part, women, to whom the knowledge of these matters was passed down from mother to daughter for countless generations. Few of them had what we would consider a formal education beyond what they had learned from their mothers and grandmothers, which set them apart from the learned profession of physicians, woefully inadequate as they were. Notwithstanding the lack of formal training, many traditional healers came to be revered and respected as important members of a village or quasi-urban community. Sometimes, of course, treatments or births went wrong, and people died, and the undereducated mob tended to lash out at providers who were supposed to be possessed of special, reliable knowledge that should have saved the unfortunate victims.

Although there were periodic localized accusations and executions for the practice of witchcraft, the Church never officially acknowledged the existence of witches (a diehard pagan belief). It wasn't until the sixteenth and seventeenth centuries that the witch-hunting hysteria really took root in Europe and the Americas. Nevertheless, there was definitely a watchfulness that societies kept on practitioners, particularly women, whose social outlook was different from their neighbors.

I thought it might be useful to imagine the existence of one particular woman who found herself participating in the life of a community, while never really belonging or feeling welcome. I imagined a woman whose background may be traced to the cultural melting pot of medieval Spain. Her scholarly father and her Jewish mother might have enriched her mind with ideas and perspectives that her new neighbors were slow and reluctant to understand or respect. What would they do when confronted with phenomena that they only dimly understood and that lent themselves to a variety of plausible explanations?

As I learned more about my characters, I began to see this work as an inquiry less into the components of any particular set of beliefs and more into the receptiveness of human nature to new ideas or cultural changes of any kind. People tend to establish around themselves a comfort zone and react irrationally towards anything that threatens its boundaries. In their suspicion of the unusual and their resistance to change, I found the people of this era not unlike those more familiar to us. I became more reluctant to condemn them in light of how our own culture has proved ready to do unspeakable things in the name of nationalism, ethnic purity, antisemitism, and islamophobia.

Man is not in need of an excuse to behave brutally toward his neighbor. He only needs to listen to the lesser angels of his nature. The story of the Witch of Bastanès became, for me, a path for understanding the journey of all of us in a world of different cultures.

The thirteenth century was also a period of rapid advancement in the development of the modern European languages that we so take for granted. Newly empowered national monarchies saw these tongues as a way of expressing something entirely their own, and the new vernacular was seen, in each case, as fit to express and transmit a heritage in poetry, philosophy, scientific inquiry, and political science. The literary schools of Province, Spain, and Sicily, as well as the enthusiasm for rendering ancient classics available, in translation, to Western scholars, are ample evidence of these stirrings. I'm certain that Michael Scot and those like him found that they were living in interesting times.

Thanks for having shared with me the lives of these people and the world they inhabited and with which they struggled.

–The Author

ABOUT THE AUTHOR

Dan Scannell is an expat American living in the south of France and visiting the U.S. His work is steeped in the culture of France, reflecting his fascination with the history of his chosen home. An accomplished author of numerous short stories, poems and essays, Dan has also been honored for his larger works of fiction.

The Fall of a Sparrow (ISBN 978-1-68433-079-9) was published in August of 2018, by Black Rose Writing. It was greeted with favorable reviews by *Indie Review*, *Readers' Favorite*, the Historical Novel Society and numerous Amazon readers. His second novel, *The Witch of Bastanes*, promises to achieve equal success because of its plot twists, colorful cast of characters and attention to language.

NOTE FROM THE AUTHOR

Word-of-mouth is crucial for any author to succeed. If you enjoyed *The Witch of Bastanès*, please leave a review online—anywhere you are able. Even if it's just a sentence or two. It would make all the difference and would be very much appreciated.

Thanks!
Dan Scannell

We hope you enjoyed reading this title from:

www.blackrosewriting.com

Subscribe to our mailing list – *The Rosevine* – and receive **FREE** books, daily deals, and stay current with news about upcoming releases and our hottest authors.
Scan the QR code below to sign up.

Already a subscriber? Please accept a sincere thank you for being a fan of Black Rose Writing authors.

View other Black Rose Writing titles at
www.blackrosewriting.com/books and use promo code
PRINT to receive a **20% discount** when purchasing.

Made in the USA
Monee, IL
07 March 2023

29379387R00121